Messages from the Sun

Messages from the Sun

encounters in elsewhen

TOM HENIGHAN

Copyright © 2018 by Tom HenighanFirst Edition

All rights reserved. No part of this book may be reproduced, stored in a retrieval system or transmitted in any form by any means—except in the case of brief quotations embodied in critical articles or reviews—without the prior written or email permission, or in the case of photocopying, a license from CANCOPY, Toronto, Ontario.

Stone Flower Press, Ottawa
Cover photo: Tom Henighan
Production Design: Jen Hamilton
Printed by CreateSpace

Library and Archives Canada Cataloguing in Publication

Henighan, Tom, author,
    Messages from the Sun/ Tom Henighan
Fiction
ISBN   978-0-9919073-5-9   (paperback)

*For the wonderfully supportive,
hugely hospitable, and greatly talented
Ottawa gang, namely, Mark and Faith,
Larry and Cara, Rick and Dale
and the faithful M*

TABLE OF CONTENTS

The Borges Transfer. 1

The Explorers. 11

The Medium. 41

Pygmalion. 57

Sargon and the Fabulous Guests. 79

Captain Flynn. 105

Locusts. 115

Massenet and the Disappearing Sopranos. 131

Rendezvous. 147

The Kosi. 185

Three Bells for Mr. Thurber. 199

Tourists from Algol. 223

Arion and the Dolphins. 247

Dream Planets. 265

Acknowledgements. 291

Thus I glimpsed from time to time another sun quite different from that by which I had been so long blessed, a sun full of the fierce dark flames of feeling, a sun of death that would never burn the skin yet gave forth a still stranger glow.

Yukio Mishima: *Sun and Steel* (1970)

The Borges Transfer

When I first discovered the works of Jorge Luis Borges, my wife and I were running out the lease of a tiny apartment convenient to the university where I was giving a series of lectures on the later developments of the theory of Socialist Realism. A few years before, we had bought a house in the country, where we enjoyed a spacious isolation and the complex pleasures of the simple life—but things soured, and our marriage nearly came apart. I was too wrapped up in my research, my wife complained, too monk-like in my intellectual discipline; she wanted me to throw myself into a concrete world of gardening and mowing. There was a comical clash of equally absurd extremes, the humour of which occurred to us only later, when we got back together after a short period of separation.

I at any rate realized then that even our break-up had been marked by that self-indulgent romanticism seemingly indispensable to our relationship. We had deceived ourselves in thinking that parting would be easy, and had tried to bedazzle ourselves with other relationships, which turned out to be only fleeting and superficial, though we found it necessary to play them up in our minds. Naturally, after such outbursts a period of recovery and truce was essential. It was beginning to be clear that almost nothing could free us from our bonds of mutual dependence, but obviously, we needed a rest.

The upshot was that after getting back together we moved into the city, storing most of our possessions, and occupying ourselves with a great deal of new work. We had spent about ten months in the apartment (which my wife had decorated with her usual ingenuity and imagination), but we finally decided to move out. Although the premises and location were nothing special, one potential renter after another appeared and was so impressed by our décor that we had trouble deciding which of them should take the lease. These strangers, clearly, had been charmed by some inimitable touches of my wife's decorating hand—too numerous and complex to mention here, although I can give you a hint by referring to a lovely antique golden birdcage, out of which she had contrived to grow the most sinuously elegant and mysteriously twining ivy.

Borges, as you probably know, is the famous South American writer who fashions those elegant brief fables that affirm the reality of art over the claims of our more mundane perceptions. To Borges, as I learned, nothing is real but the imagination: what we imagine becomes the truth in the most literal and sometimes ironic sense, as when a set of complex mathematical equations become simplified in a bomb. This writer had been recommended to my wife by one of her lovers, I think, during our separation, and in normal circumstances this might have been enough to put me off, but under the tense conditions of our marital truce, it made reading him almost more piquant.

In a little while I had devoured almost everything available by the great Argentine, and while my wife continued to read almost nothing but murder mysteries, I had learned to appreciate touches like that in his story "Tlön, Uqbar, Orbis Tertius," in which a country is created that exists only so long as it is imagined. In this story, doorways and amphitheatres disappear when there is no one to think about them. Was Borges really a philosophical idealist, or was he subtly hinting at the existence of worlds that remain invisible because no one has yet imagined them for us? Did this mean that our familiar world too might become invisible, when imagination failed to renew our intimate connections with it?

Now at the time that I was being led to consider these questions, one of the potential renters of our tiny apartment signed a lease, and we were free to move elsewhere. With a certain enthusiasm we decided to pursue our old preference for large houses with complex floor plans and extra space that seemed to serve no earthly use. We moved only a dozen blocks away, but to a house many times the size of our apartment. I remember that after packing our things for the movers we stopped, quite exhausted, at a local restaurant, where, in a mood of intimate, relaxed goodwill, I explained to my wife the plot of one of Borges' most famous tales, "The Library of Babel." In this story, the writer conceives of the whole universe as a vast library, and imagines many strange touches, such as people wandering endlessly through it, never able to master all of the texts, and sometimes disappearing after years of searching for even a single book that, among all those millions, might be identical with another one.

That night my wife and I slept in our newly rented house for the first time. We had made the arrangements with an old Italian woman, whose ad we had found in a local paper that ceased publication soon after. It seemed incredibly fortuitous. Finding decent housing in that particular area of town was always a difficult prospect, yet we had chanced on a huge house at a very reasonable rent, in a remarkably short time.

True, there were problems with the place. It must have been occupied previously by extremely untidy hippie students, for it was very dirty and unkempt, and furthermore always seemed somewhat dark, no matter how we arranged the lighting. It was also vast. On the first night we slept on the third floor, listening to the great spaces of perhaps twenty (or was it thirty?) rooms reverberating around us with sharp but meaningless sounds. Lying there on a mattress on the floor, I was sorry I had not picked up that plate from downstairs, which seemed to have sat on a dusty window ledge for centuries, its cargo of chicken bones picked over more than once by mice or rats. I was also very sorry that my wife's golden birdcage with its trailing ivy had been damaged amid our upheaval. I had last seen it (in which room I forgot), the ivy drooping and faltering in the dull yellow light of that hectic evening, and I thought of it just as I finally drifted vaguely into a kind of lazy, half-disturbed sleep.

The next morning, when I woke up, I noticed with some surprise that my wife was already up and gone. Usually I had to wake her, to send her off to the government office she worked in—she was a heavy sleeper. But now, the hollow groans and odd reverberations of the old house told me that I was alone in all of its creaking spaces. I was at first somewhat nonplussed, but soon recovered my equanimity, and picked up yet another volume of Borges to while away the time before I would have to do some work on my lectures. It was then that I read his essay "A New Refutation of Time," in which he seems to argue from the extreme position of the philosophical idealist: time is an illusion; we live only in the present; matter per se is an absurdity. Mind is the endlessly creative medium, and all literature becomes, for those who care to practise it, an act of identification. Thus, the fervent reader of Shakespeare becomes Shakespeare, the avid reader of Dante *is* Dante. And even these great names become almost insignificant in the still greater overworld that is the language system itself, every possible story repeated forever, with endless variations, across the distances of time, to make up a universe of discourse, magnificent and terrifying as the galaxies....

Was it really days later when I next saw my wife? The strange shadows of the house gave everything a dreamlike air and made all such conclusions uncertain. We sat silently, with almost nothing to say to each other. I had no inclination to tell her any more about Borges. I was not surprised when she wandered away upstairs without even saying good night.

On another such evening, when she seemed to have gone to bed, I decided that I wanted to explore the whole labyrinthine reality of the house. I took a flashlight with me and began to wander through it, probing about the damp, fetid basement, where much of our luggage from the country had been piled for later sorting and unpacking. There was a curious quality I noticed here, which went on striking me as I attempted to make my way through the whole house. In every room, something specific would catch my eye, or intrigue me, so that I would almost forget the purpose of my tour and stay there, for hours it seemed, wrapped up in aimless reveries.

These excursions went on night after night, and

on one of them I remember that I found a strange old book, thick with dust, lying in a corner of the basement. It was half-hidden underneath a small box of frankincense and myrrh I had brought back from Arabia many years before. When I picked it up and started to look at it, however, the book seemed to fly out of my hands: it was a single long page folded up like a fan and set between two wooden boards. When you opened it upward from left to right, seemingly the wrong way, you could see quaint modem paintings representing certain Chinese sages and scholars, accompanied by sayings from their works. If you tried to open it in the usual way, however, turning the cover upward from right to left, you found a book with pages that were utterly blank. I couldn't remember ever buying this book, and was sure I had never seen it before. Either it was a recent acquisition of my wife's that she had forgotten to mention to me, or else it had been left behind by some unknown earlier tenant.

I must have sat for hours over this book, setting it up on a table like a child's house of cards, turning the pages in both directions, studying the curious detail of the drawings—the enigmatic smiles of the sages, the landscapes of trees and flowers receding into the distance. And soon certain of the phrases and sayings began to haunt my mind, mixing themselves up with the sentences of some Borges story or essay, so that as I walked slowly up and down the corridors I seemed to hear a blur of secret, mixed accents, cautioning me about illusions, about the chasms and distances between any single word and the next....

That was a long time ago, I think. I must bravely tell you the truth, which I know you have been expecting, and will accept: I have not recently, in all my wanderings and searchings through this vastly complex labyrinth of rooms, met my wife. The house, it seems, is endless, as I discover anew each day, or hour, or minute, of my inspection. Floor after floor unfolds, bearing a slight resemblance to something I well remember, but remaining utterly alien. I have ambled now, possibly for ages, up and down those narrow stairs, sleeping on an odd mattress I chanced to find in some half-disordered corner, my ears attentive for the least sound of an approaching familiar voice, but always disappointed, for everything I hear seems to be the echo of my own footsteps, or the amplified energies of my own breathing, which grows more and more distinct in the absolute silence around me. Just once, I wandered into a long dark corridor, indistinguishable from all the rest, on a floor I can't really remember, and I thought I saw, in the faint daylight, a clear girlish face peering at me anxiously from behind a half-open door. I moved closer at once, my heart beating rather wildly (I couldn't say why), but found that the girl had vanished. Perhaps I will meet her again, if she really lives here, or perhaps she is someone who dropped in by mistake and is gone now, though her face will register with me forever, like a flash of white alabaster beneath a dusty half-parted curtain. Perhaps (who knows?) I mistook her completely, and it was my wife looking for me in these endless spaces, through all these infinitely gloomy rooms, even as I continue to look for her, trying to remember, minute by minute, what it was I wanted to say to her, as a last, most important communication from the silence of my own heart.

But all I can be sure of as I sit here, in this unfamiliar room, reading yet one more story by the master Borges, is that the last faint twirls of ivy have climbed back into the golden birdcage, and seem locked up forever in the dull light shining from one corner of this house, which has finally become the whole universe for me.

The Explorers

On the last expedition, just before the end of the world, they set out to find the Yeti.

The Yeti had been known to most of them for a long time, but none of them had ever seen it. Each had been acquainted with someone who made that claim, but all they could put together between them were seventeen footprints, a black shape bounding across the snow one hundred yards distant, and a collection of dubious old bones.

Their leader, Lord Hutton, a ruddy-faced man of great strength who remembered Thesiger, invited them to his estate in Northumberland to talk it over. Foucault, the philosopher and Alpine climber, couldn't come; he had fallen over a tree stump in his yard and had sprained his ankle. His apology arrived in a telegram just as Evans left Manchester, bringing with him some photographs sent to him from Nepal only a few months before. Sir Harry Groves was in London picking up his fees as a bit player in the new epic, *Film Without Humour,* which several directors had agreed to collaborate on. This movie was supposed to explore the nature of the serious, although a few contended (supported by Sir Harry in casual conversation) that the serious had no nature; it was simply the condition of being without humour, which explained why it was such a difficult mode to sustain. Sir Harry arrived first, eager for news.

"What the devil is Colin up to?" was the way Chuck Legg put it to himself when he got Hutton's letter at his ranch house outside of Taos, New Mexico. Like the rest of them he was rather old, seventy-seven to be exact, and the transatlantic routes, even supposing he had been close to them, were very dangerous during this period of phony war just before the final send-up.

"I'm for it," was what he said when he finished the letter.

The drawing room at Peak House was lovely. Originally by Adam, it had been salvaged and reassembled by Lord Hutton's grandfather when the northeast coast of England had drifted away in a storm one winter. Actually, the old boy had been after the Durham Cathedral door knocker, but the room was a find nonetheless, and it had been worked in around the existing fireplace, roaring now with a kindly ancient warmth.

The first thing they did was to look at the Evans photographs. Some of them had tears in their eyes as they examined the blank white nothingness of snow.

"South col of Kanchenjunga," Sir Harry was not slow to affirm.

"Bloody impressive shot," Lord Hutton added.

"Looks like footprints in the foreground, for sure," suggested Legg, who had made it over on Pan Am.

"Wait until you see the close-ups," Evans concluded, delighted at this response.

For the non-aficionado a word of description should be added, for how many, other than CIA spies, extreme sport fanatics, Chicom infiltrators, and TV Eyewitness News cameramen have trekked those forbidden spaces?

As one inspired traveler put it: *the colossal mountain mass soared up to a giddy height—to the ethereal workshops in which the eternal snow spins the delicate webs which it sends down the slopes of the mountain as offerings to the sun, where the winds gambol at their will, and where the stillness of death divides sovereignty with the bitter cold.*

The next photograph (actually a colour slide) showed clearly some mighty strange-looking footprints.

The footprints could have been made by a Yeti. The group looked on in silence. These were experienced explorers; they refused to jump to conclusions, but they were profoundly moved. After several more pictures, a council of war was held over some cognac.

It was then and there agreed to launch a new expedition. Conditions were far from ideal, as Lord Hutton was quick to point out. The world was trembling on the verge. Travel was becoming increasingly difficult and expensive. Government assistance was out of the question.

Lord Hutton stood a few feet from the fire; his weathered old face became a grotesque mask in the flickering light. Hands clenched into fists, he surveyed his comrades with a slightly squinting affection.

"Well, lads, are we for it?"

The answer was evident in each man's hearty

affirmation.

During the next few days, orders went out in many directions, to Fortnum and Mason, Abercrombie and Fitch, Black's, White's, Green's, Bhicajee Cowasjee, and to sundry other surprised suppliers in the more elegant districts of London, New York, and Delhi.

The orders came back with all speed. They made up the usual freight of such adventures: ropes, skis, boots, pitons, the Bible, and various kinds of expensive cameras. Nothing was wrapped in brown paper. The oxygen masks were the latest models, the Sherpas the oldest hands, to be contracted on the spot.

At the first base of Katmandu, the three Englishmen and the American waited for Foucault, who had promised to join them, but did not appear. Supposing that he was a casualty of the accelerating violence, they made their plans without him. Their assumption was not entirely wrong. Forced into an unaccustomed idleness by his sprained ankle, Foucault had become aware that his young wife was being unfaithful to him, and that in fact she had been deceiving him for years. Greatly disturbed, but exercising splendid self-control, he fell back upon his philosophy of tragic acceptance, learned from Nietzsche, to which he added the idea drawn from

Freud through Lacan that the concrete had to be taken precisely for what it was: the concrete. He regretted of course that in the case of his wife his perceptions of the real had led him astray, and he also lamented this interruption in his pursuit of the Yeti, which he had hoped to study as a species of linguistic exotica, without any metaphysical preconceptions. Nonetheless, he proceeded to Paris to complete the purchase of supplies and to give a paper on "The Self-Sufficiency of the Now" at the nine thousand seven hundred twenty-fifth meeting of the European Psychoanalytic Association, only to be caught directly in the first major exchange of nuclear rockets between the Americans and the Chinese. Strolling near the Jardin du Luxembourg, he heard the sinister alarms and watched the skyline of the city erupt in the splendour of a dazzling pink-white halo of fire.

"Revolution!" he cried, shaking his fist at this telltale apocalypse of oppression, and refusing to run for the Métro. He was struck down where he stood by an enormous wave of heat, which his senses translated under shock into a cold breath blown straight from the remotest Himalayan heights.

Katmandu, not without its own past troubles, was far removed from the terrible accidents of the period of nuclear confrontation. While a temporary peace ensued and negotiations went furiously forward in the world capitals (apologies being made for the mistake that killed several millions), the explorers, virtually self-sufficient, decided to cross over into Tibet in order to begin their search. At Sangsang, in sight of the venerable Brahmaputra River, they recruited porters and prepared to work back into the Himalayan chain, following the caravan routes and riverbeds and moving upward steadily into the great glacial highlands, which they already knew from many years past.

Foucault's presumed death was a sad burden to them in the early stages of the trip, but under the influence of the awesome landscape, even such a sharp loss must fall into place. They set out through bright April weather, following the cold glitter of a nameless stream toward the cloudless peaks. Low hills coiled before them, dark flexed flanks of the mighty massif. A few villages of sprawling huts housed them en route, or they camped under the steep shelter of cliffs, watching the sky for signs of a change in the weather. Struggling across a giant spur of the central ranges, they felt themselves hauled up by encircling arms. It was as if they stood still while the mountains slowly engulfed them.

In time that was no time they found themselves skirting bright glaciers that seemed poised and tilted forever under a wedge of sky.

In the middle of the third week, a storm drove down upon them from the heights as they prepared to camp. Darkness came on quickly, and the snow whirled about them, polished to sinister brilliance by the angled last light. Hurriedly, they urged the ponies in toward the rim of a sheltering valley. The storm broke over the valley, a careless fury of edges cutting and tearing at their half-anchored haven. They crouched under improvised shelters as the night passed wearily.

At noon of the next day the storm abated, but there was trouble with the porters. Four of them refused to go farther, claiming that their dreams had collectively predicted disaster for the expedition. Lord Hutton, questioning them closely, could learn nothing more. It was decided that Chuck Legg would accompany the Tibetans to the nearest village and attempt to recruit replacements there.

As he was preparing to leave, the weather brightened, and Legg unpacked his treasured pearl-handled revolvers from the baggage and strapped them under his weatherproofs. The pistols, which he had acquired while he was adviser to one of the Oman oil sheikhs, were a kind of good luck charm. All the while he had worn them he had made vast sums of money, which enabled him to buy several thousand acres in the vicinity of Lobo Mountain, New Mexico. There he had established various enterprises as his tastes changed: an experimental sexual recreation centre, a library of books by and about Immanuel Velikovsky, and a farm and factory to produce goat's milk cheese. Lean and rugged, his reflexes as quick as ever despite his years, Legg followed the four mounted ex-porters—whose names happened to be Barkha, Tokchen, Shamstang, and Sersok—down the dim trail that stretched away through many yawning valleys to the town of Kampak. On the way he practised several Tibetan dialects, discussing the afterlife and attempting to translate sentences from *Alice in Wonderland*, which the porters took to be a sacred text. After three days they reached the village, but, alas, no replacements were to be found there. Disappointed, Legg said goodbye to the four and started back. On the second day, halfway up a steep mountain climb, he came upon a surprising sight: a tent made of black yak's hair, its anchoring thongs singing and creaking in the rather stiff wind. Inside he found a nomad and his wife eating a dinner of nettle spinach. Politely they welcomed him and offered him a bowl of tasty barley beer. The effect of this brew was stronger than the explorer had remembered. After a while the woman's dark eyes seemed to glitter with a faintly mocking light. She offered to read his palm and told him he would never find the Yeti. But he had not mentioned the Yeti to them—or had he? The effects of the beer made it difficult to remember.

The next day the man invited him to go hunting. Legg was anxious to test his revolvers. Riding out, they saw only some wild sheep vanishing over a distant rocky ridge. Legg fired a few shots, but the targets were well out of range. The report crashed and echoed across the mountain slopes. The Tibetan was delighted. His round wrinkled face eager, he hauled out his own weapon, a clumsy antique muzzleloader, and let out a blast that seemed to shout back at them from all the ravines. Legg rocked in his saddle, surprised and amused at the weapon. He asked if he might examine it, and was just sitting down to do so when he heard a sudden faint roaring from far above. A vague intuition suggested to him what it was. He shouted to the Tibetan, clambered up on his mount, and galloped off as fast as the pony would take him. The Tibetan did not move.

Legg stopped for a moment and cried out—he was trying to warn the fellow, shouting and pointing. The Tibetan did not move. In despair Legg reached for one of his revolvers and fired it quickly into the air, stirring up the sluggish pony and making him run. In a few precious seconds he had got the pony trotting at a good speed. The poor beast seemed terrified. Legg leaned down over the animal's neck and stole a look back at the Tibetan, who was staring at him in astonishment, not moving at all. *The poor fool*, Legg was thinking, *the poor fool.*

It was one of his last thoughts that trip out. The crazed pony found its footwork useless in mid-air: stumbling out of stride, it had pitched forward across the edge of a thousand-foot crevasse, taking its astounded rider with it.

The next morning, sunrise was spectacular. Waking up in their tent, the Tibetan and his wife were inclined to ascribe the display to their strange guest, whom the hunter had seen with his own eyes fly off into the region of the eternal spirits.

2

The explorers waited two weeks for the missing Legg, sending out two of the remaining porters in search of him, only to find that neither news nor the porters returned. A series of sunrises and sunsets of spectacular coloration led them to believe that another nuclear holocaust might be in progress, and, saddened though they were by the disappearance of their friend, they determined to push on. Now that civilization as they had known it was ending, they might as well continue their quest.

In another week, during which there were no more portents in the sky, they reached the Valley of Katchanga with their five remaining porters and made the first significant discovery of the expedition.

While digging up some snow to be boiled for water, Yengla, one of the porters, discovered a large and mysterious footprint etched in the hard pack at the protected base of a large boulder. Wild with excitement, the three explorers crowded round.

"Not human," Evans asserted, peering down at it.

"Not animal, either," Hutton assured them, scrambling over with one of the cameras.

"Gentlemen," Groves solemnly announced, "we've discovered the eighteenth known footprint of the Yeti." He went to work at once, taking measurements, casts, and endless photographs.

They were sure there must be more prints, but

after three days and a thorough search of the area for miles around, they had found nothing. It was difficult not to be disappointed. Regretfully, they agreed they must split up. Groves insisted on staying to continue the search for footprints in the many caves at the other end of the valley. Yengla would remain with him, while the other porters would go with Hutton and Evans.

When his friends had taken leave, Groves moved his camp to the largest of the caves, a narrow black slash in the snow-encrusted side of the valley. Inside, the cave was more spacious, stretching back into a ribbed gloom of branching archways. With the help of Yengla, Groves built a low wall of loose stones across the mouth of the cave as a windbreak, and they gathered brushwood for the cooking fire and set their belongings in order. The next day the exploration of the caves began, starting with the one in which they had camped. They traced two passages to impenetrable fissures in the remote recesses of the rock, marked out trails, and returned. The third passage was more interesting, because it branched into two farther ones, and one of these into two farther ones. At the end of a week a whole series of caves had been marked out for further investigation. It was then that the extraordinary pink sunrises and sunsets began again. Yengla, who had heard the explorers talk about the end of the world, insisted on taking a week off to go to the nearest village, where he hoped to send a message to his family. Groves continued the exploration of the caves on his own.

Groves swung his burly frame through cavern after cavern, twirling his splendid old-fashioned moustache and reciting lines from all the various films he had played bit parts in as he mugged shamelessly to the nonexistent cameras. From time to time he mouthed passages from Tibullus or Horace or listened to his digital recording of the *Aeneid*, delivered in Latin by himself, and the close and fetid air boomed with the sonorous ancient melodies of Aeneas' descent into Avernus

Groves had graduated from classics at Cambridge to films at Ealing, returning at intervals to his Norfolk birthplace, where he had stored his splendid collection of first editions of the works of his ancestor, H. Rider Haggard. His dreams of making the ultimate film version of *She* had been interrupted in turn by the economic crisis resulting from decades of negative climate change, the nuclear exchanges, and the urgent call from Lord Hutton to join his final attempt to locate the elusive Yeti. Alas, now he feared, and rightly, that the *She* project would disappear into the limbo of unrealized wishes. Nonetheless, as he sat back with his pipe every evening beside the fire, he worked meticulously over the script, building the lost city of Kor out of the thousand separate scenes he had so painstakingly imagined from the original text.

It was a few days after the departure of Yengla that Groves made his discovery. He was re-thinking the cave scene in *She* in which Billali shows Horace Holly the relic of the woman's foot. He was wondering whether he should insert a flashback to convey the burning of the woman's corpse or rely on Billali's narrative, and his mind was so full of vivid pictures rapidly shuffled that at first he missed the amazing spoor at the mouth of the deep left-branching cave, which he had so far barely explored.

It was a footprint that leapt to life in the beam of the torch, and he had missed it on his earlier foray because it was imprinted on a small ledge or shelf of stone. He stopped and stared down at it now, his breath coming fast with excitement. Another single mysterious footprint, larger than a man's, belonging to no known species of ape or bear, a footprint stamped not on the bare rock but on the softer, more recently mud-caked surface of the stone. The nineteenth known footprint of the Yeti, here in this very cave!

The next few hours were spent in furious and meticulous recording of the evidence. Photographs in colour and black and white, another cast, the taking of some samples for laboratory analysis—when all this was finally done, Groves collapsed in fitful and exhausted sleep, determined that on the next day he would penetrate the left-branching system of caves in search of further clues.

After breakfast and a walk through the valley to take the air, Groves took one last look at the sinister pink of the dawn, then began his descent into the deeper recesses of the mountain.

Loaded down with knapsack and ropes, reflecting metallic markers, a camera, a tape recorder, and even a special gun equipped with a hypodermic needle, Groves penetrated farther and farther into the caves. Wearing a miner's headlamp and a light strapped to his belt, he edged along grim corridors of stone not seen previously, perhaps, by any human eyes. Alas, no camera crew followed, no network distribution, only his own voice-over burst forth moment by moment in a curse or a song. Gone were the endless spaces of Himalayan grandeur, gone were the peaks and the shining glaciers; he had succeeded in burying himself in a single tiny crack of those great ranges.

Time passed, progress was slow—it was difficult to make a thorough search along every inch of passageway. Perhaps that was why Groves became only slowly aware of that odd subterranean rumbling, a murmur sounding a level deeper than he had so far penetrated, a vague distant bubbling somewhere below him. He stopped and listened, then crouched in a space where the cave wall met the floor in a cracked and pitted shelf. He put his ear there, listening, and smelled the rising dampness, like some ancient impersonal rot in the stone itself. He heard the sound of waters flowing away endlessly in the darkness far beneath him. As he struggled to his feet, mentally dazed by this experience, and bending under the weight of his heavy pack, his light flashed on the strange cocoon-like bundles hanging down from a jutting finger of rock on the cave wall opposite.

He stood in his tracks, gasping, noticing that the objects had been carefully strung along the cave wall. He counted them: thirteen in all. He moved to get at the first one, eager to touch it, to tear it open (it looked a bit like a dark haunch of ham, he thought), then caught himself. Carefully unpacking his cameras, he photographed everything in sight. Only then did reach for the first of the bundles.

It was a parcel of the softest lambskin. Inside was a single nearly blackened leg of smoked goat's meat. He unpacked the bundles, one by one. In each was a single leg of the goat's meat, in the same state of crumbling half-decay—in each except the last. When he examined the last, he was so excited it seemed his pounding heart might beat its way out through his chest. Inside the last skin was a small flat object carefully wrapped in an opaque plastic cover. The plastic, which seemed quite new, was folded in at the edges. Before he unwrapped it, his trembling fingers already knew what it contained. Surely—but quite unaccountably—it was a book.

He turned it over, reading the title again and again, absolutely dumbfounded. Then he began to laugh. His laughter increased in volume and spread through the cave like a wild magnetic current. Soon it seemed that the laughter was not his but the cave's, the hidden river's, that the laughter itself had pursued him for a long time, only to catch him out then and there. Now it went on and on, his hand shook, and he dropped the book. It lay at his feet, an ordinary paperback edition of Lobsang Rampa's *The Third Eye*.

3

It was weeks later when Yengla brought Lord Hutton and Evans the news of the disappearance of Harry Groves. He had tracked the explorer everywhere, he affirmed—even into the deepest caves—and found nothing, no trace of the man, his camp, or of the two ponies Groves had kept with him after Yengla's departure.

A gloom settled over the camp, and for the first time in his life the normally imperturbable Hutton began to entertain fears of ultimate failure. Everything, it seemed, was ending at last; all the possibilities imagined as part of the world they had known would have to remain unrealized.

After a few days of indecision, they agreed to continue their northwestward trek, detouring slightly where necessary to obtain some news of events in the world outside.

The day before their departure Hutton undertook a climb up the Malduk. They had made their camp far below a labyrinth of moraine ridges, pyramids, and ice-clefts that sprang out of a great steel-blue glacier on the mountain's southern flanks. Hutton climbed up toward the Kamruk glacier, which he had explored ten years before as part of a vain effort to reach the summit. On that expedition his closest friend, Ismail, a Circassian, had fallen to his death when a rope broke a few thousand feet from the very top. The body was never found.

Hutton, six foot five and proportionately muscled, a former amateur boxing champion, had studied mathematics in Berlin and was the first experimenter to run the test devised by A.M. Turing to determine whether the then most advanced series of computers could be said to think. The tests proved inconclusive, and the world ban on ultra-automation diverted work on super-intelligent machines into secret projects, the results of which were so far unknown. It occurred to Hutton, however, that the pattern of international breakdown experienced during the last several months had something predictable and almost mathematical about it. It might be that men had secretly decided, or been secretly compelled, to program Armageddon, leaving nothing to chance or the mercies of human improvisation.

It was because of his interest in the ultra-intelligent computer that Hutton had been led in pursuit of the Yeti. He had felt that if man had already proved that there was a further evolutionary stage beyond him, that of the machine, or solid state intelligence, it might throw additional light on his nature if it could be proved also that there was a stage behind him, in the direction of the animal kingdom from which *Homo sapiens* had partially emerged. To Hutton, the Yeti was a possible missing link in the metaphysical chain that led from unthinking matter to fully-autonomous thinking machines.

As the day passed and Hutton continued his climb, he knew that he must spend a night on the mountain, to commune with the spirits of his dead companions and to rethink some of the assumptions that had occupied him through an active and productive life. On a small outcropping of rock that fenced the glacier gorge on his right, he leveled the ground and set up his tent. Far below, the glacier tongues and lakes were already darkening, the wind stirred, and he was glad of the shelter of the few schist boulders around him as he prepared to face the oncoming night.

He had expected a picturesque sunset, but that evening it was nothing out of the ordinary. The sun sank into clouds illumined by a fiery yellow flare that glowed for a long time after the sun had gone down and threw all the surrounding peaks into sharp relief. Soon his tent was shrouded in darkness.

For a moment the very top of Malduk glittered almost as if it were an active volcano, and then the light of day was swallowed up entirely.

Hutton walked out to see the full moon rise and watched it dim the stars, which only moments before had glittered so fiercely. It was not so far, after all, to the boundless realms of space. The moon rose like a burnished silver shield sailing up from the black perpendicular wall of the glacier's near defile. Everything was silent except for the occasional dull crack of a newly forming crevasse or the crash of an avalanche tumbling down suddenly from an ice mantle higher up. It was very cold, but not punishing.

Hutton took from his pocket the book that he carried with him everywhere, a battered old copy, bound in a protective jacket, of *My View of the World*, by the twentieth-century physicist, Schrödinger. Hutton had no need to open it to the passage he wanted, for he knew it by heart. It was Schrödinger, on a mountain in the Alps, confessing to himself the truth of Vedanta, that the moment was eternal, that he had always been just there and would never be anywhere else, that change was the real illusion and not permanence.

The great explorer fixed his gaze upward and

outward at the moon and the silver peaks. He felt that he was already a vast distance from the earth. If he stood there long enough and patiently enough, the avalanches would thunder down toward him but never reach him, the mountain would shift and change but stay fixed in place, the Yeti would be discovered and yet continue to be a mystery.

As the moon rose ever higher—rises ever higher—Lord Hutton is turning to point a mittened hand at the darkness. He is remembering how he once watched two Tibetan monks release the spirit of a dying man, using those powerful magical exclamations that would send the immaterial soul flying into its next rebirth. *Perhaps the world itself is now in need of just such a release.* If he concentrates his mind and utters the magical words, standing there on that high ledge in those great spaces saturated by moonlight, perhaps he can ease the dying planet's death agony and send everything whirling off into another dimension of space and time.

Hands raised high, Lord Hutton makes some signs in the air. He is trying very hard to concentrate the whole power of his mind.

"HIK PHAT!" he cries out, the words of the ritual exploding in his throat.

"HIK PHAT!"

Above him and around him the glacier dissolves and condenses like a sinister plasma....

4

A week later, Evans, quite alone, struggles on through a snowy wasteland. Every now and then he stops to fire a gun into the air, he stops to take a photograph, he stops to laugh at nothing, he stops to think.

Evans the handyman, Evans the relative of Scott's doughty companion, must remain undaunted by every circumstance. For days the skies had been full of green and gold and violet menace, the menace of unnatural beauty, and there had been no rumours, because he had met no one, but rumours were now unnecessary. There was a peculiar stillness, a curious lack of vibration in the air that possibly told the story. And the strange cloud shapes of unnatural fire. And the body of a Tibetan shepherd in his tent, his features twisted hideously out of shape, as if he had looked on that unnatural fire. And the footprints everywhere, the footprints that Evans must follow higher and higher into the mountains, footprints that were neither man nor known animal, the twentieth, twenty-first, twenty-second, and twenty-third attested footprints of the Yeti.

He walked on, and somewhere along the way, Evans thought to himself: *It's curious that I'm here. That I'm the one who's been chosen to carry on.*

But carry on he did, remembering his days in the navy, as an engineer on H.M.S. *Cobra*, sailing past the lovely harsh island of Socotra, thinking about dragon's blood trees and writing letters to his wife and four children back in Bristol. His family must be gone now, everything must be gone, but one had to do one's duty, one had to continue. It probably wasn't the fault of the machines, as some people thought. It wasn't anybody's fault. It was predestined, all of this. And besides, it was never the end. There were always a few left over, to start the whole thing up again.

He chewed away on his last remaining plug of tobacco, ate a chocolate bar or two sometime later, and took a swig of brandy from the hip flask. As far as he knew he was headed south toward India, over the last high peaks of the Himalayas. There was no way, of course, that he could make it, now that Hutton was gone and the porters had all deserted. But he had to go on anyway.

He came at last to a high valley in the Himalayan foothills, a broad spacious valley where the weather was milder and the snow was beginning to melt. With his food gone and his mind confused by sheer motion and by his reflections on the depressing events of the expedition, Evans's will to live was sinking rapidly, despite the easier circumstances of travel. That night he had no strength to set up his tent. He lay down in the snow, well realizing that to fall asleep unsheltered in those temperatures would probably mean death.

The next morning he was surprised to see how much better he felt. He opened his eyes on the clear sunlit day, on a sky of blue splendour. He tried to sit up.

Then he noticed that in attempting to sit up he had somehow propelled himself up and away not only from the earth, but from his own body, which lay there inert and seemingly lifeless in the drifting, melting snow.

How curious it was to stare down at his own dead body, to see himself for the first time when he was really no longer himself! He regarded his mortal husk with tender love and pity and wondered if he would ever again inhabit that frail carcass.

Then, slowly, like a child learning to walk, he stepped across the snow, out and away from the scene of his own apparent death.

THE EXPLORERS

He moved easily across the brilliant landscape, not wanting to wander too far, wondering just what he might do next. He had heard of people who had somehow become detached from their bodies, but of course they had always managed to climb back on board, so as to tell the tale. But if he ventured back into that seeming derelict, he wondered, would this bright feeling vanish? Would he be dead and obliterated once and for all, trapped in the deep frozen hulk that such a short time before he had treasured as his dearest possession?

Since he did not know what to do he merely stayed there, keeping watch on his own body, and soon he noticed a very curious thing. Somehow time itself had shifted and become distorted, because as he waited and watched, day and night began to alternate in a strange rhythm that seemed to have nothing to do with the world as he remembered it, but which responded directly to what he felt in his own mind. Before long he was making the sun and moon dance forward in crazy rhythms that were both dizzying and altogether delightful.

The next time he looked down at his own late body it had changed beyond recognition. For one thing it was much longer, at least seven or eight feet tall. Then too it had grown a thick coat of hair, a warm fur that seemed to have burst out of the crumpled and rotted clothing and that shone with vitality and health. His fingernails and toenails had become sharp curved claws on powerful extremities. His arms were longer and reached to his knees. His ears lay close to his skull, which was larger and squarer, a huge cranium covered with glossy fur.

He knew that now he could enter his body again, and he did so without fear. He lay down inside himself and became one with what he had become.

When he got up, he sensed that everything had fallen back into something like the rhythms he vaguely remembered. At the same time, it was very different. He stretched his arms and felt the power surge through them to the sharp curves of his magnificent claws. He could see the snow in a thousand subtle variations of line and texture. When he moved he covered the ground easily in powerful strides, and when he ran he barely touched it, bounding from place to place with an energy he drew from contact with the earth itself.

Time passed and he learned to run on the highest peaks, to cross the glaciers, to reach the caves far back in the mountains where he could exchange knowledge without words with others of his kind. Slowly, he forgot almost all of the past. He lived in the present exclusively, in the strength of his seemingly tireless pleasure.

Only once, a long time later, did he meet any creature other than his own kind, or come upon any animal other than sheep or yak, wolf, antelope, or bear. He was striding across a great ridge below Nanda Devi when he happened suddenly upon a medium-sized animal slipping and sliding awkwardly across the rock in tiny, timid steps. The creature, wrapped tightly in its protective garments, peered at him with a sharp and metallic gaze from behind something it wore over its face. Even in his quick sideways glance, and despite the masked face, he sensed at once its sharp curiosity, the cold hunger of its stare, the anxious struggle in that intruder between fear and awe and violence.

He bounded away gladly, leaving behind only a faint track of footprints that the wind came down and obliterated one by one.

The Medium

Inside the cabin, lulled by the pleasant piped-in music, Dr. S., the well-known television scientist, dozes and waits for the miracle of flight. He is thinking, perhaps for no reason at all, of a fox he once saw at dusk on the farm of a friend. The fox, sharp red against the spring green foliage, turned for an instant to look at him just before it vanished into the gathering shadows. That look, he knew, was the inside-out of nature, and he couldn't read it. He had forgotten such looks in taking stock of the glances, rubbery or brittle, directed at him daily by his fellow humans. They recognized him, of course, but couldn't always remember from where. And soon he waited for and was amused by that recognition, partial or otherwise. He even missed it when it was lacking for more than a few hours, though it seldom was, because he spent most of his time these days and nights on airplanes, between engagements, most of his life in the functional plush of cabins exactly like this, or in the functional clutter of studios. (From there you looked at nature outside-in, hoping to catch the gleam in the eye of the fox.)

Now the engines of the plane roar well and truly; there is a slight shiver and, barely perceptible, the hoarse mechanical whisper of hidden parts. The attendants have been busy, assisting a spastic, handing out newspapers and candy, unpacking food and drink. They have noticed their notable passenger obliquely, if at all. Eyeing his briefcase, Dr. S. sighs and prepares to take aim at his scripts. Concentration, however, does not come. The plush cabin soothes, without releasing, the stranded senses. A moment's self-reflection, with ominous logic, beams up Narcissus. Dr. S. mentally retraces his steps through the waiting room, past the boarding desk, and into his seat, re-arranging the fleeting faces to restore a pattern from which he can mentally check out all the various reactions to his own presence. At the same time, he is struggling with one part of his mind to remember how Bohm's use of the hologram illustrates the notion of implicate order, that order out of which everything that is emerges. Dr. S. reaches for his briefcase. SCIENCE EXPLAINS. (Why hadn't he followed that fox into the woods, he wondered? Perhaps the sharp glance was a warning. But of what? His own dog, Quantum, was incapable of such a glance. In the strictest sense, Quantum was hardly "natural" at all.)

The plane sits poised in its loop of space-time, shuddering, then, at the peak of its shudder, rolls forward. A sudden thrust, a steepening angle of climb. They are strung now on a line of invisible points and headed west for the City of the Angels. Why is it, Dr. S. asks himself, that I always think of death at these moments of absolutely routine miracle? He swallows very hard, his body tense and straining upward as if to fly out of the coffin that the plane might become. As usual, he recognizes the ironies of all deaths accompanied by bad food, second-rate movies, and superficial conversation. But the roar reassures, the angle of climb becomes normal. A few moments more and there is a general release of tension, a general rush to fall into the lazy banalities of travel.

Up the wide aisle, suddenly, myopically, trots none other than Harmon Yablonski, the famous neurological specialist from McGill. The famous neurological specimen, thinks Dr. S., watching the nervous flutter of hands, the jerk of the shoulders. Yet S. responds amiably, automatically, to his colleague's curt nod, with a benevolent, bare-toothed smile.

Suddenly the aisle is nearly crowded; the captain's blurred voice has just dispensed from above a few facts about the weather and altitude. Orange-red sunlight enters a tangle of bodies edging gently tailward, giving their movement an air of intention, as if they were dancing. (And this environment, our world, when you think about it, Dr. S. concludes, is one that tries to simulate order, if only to pretend to banish all chance. It is precisely the opposite of the forest path, where the fox may suddenly turn and look at you, for no reason you could easily fathom. And even if some crazy fanatic sits in the third seat forward with bombs strapped to his belly or testicles, the machinery that works against him, however crude, will be relentless, and quite predictable. Which is the beauty of human society, and its terror).

Dr. S. has scribbled some of this in his personal notebook. The innocuous-looking lady in the green blouse who sits across the aisle leans over.

"Haven't I seen you on the Oprah show?" she

asks. "Or on *Nova*?"

Her confusion of him with Deepak Chopra, Bill Nye, or Carl Sagan settled, she turns the talk to the most recent issue of *Astrology Today*, which she carries in a very large string bag, with some oranges and her knitting. Her interest in quarks and quasars is certainly limited, but she is anxious to talk about the stars. She tells him she is Mrs. Fox from Cincinnati.

Dr. S. orders another drink and turns to his neighbour on the left. This turns out to be merely a Mr. Neumann from Des Moines, solid and red-faced, brusquely shifting pages of the *Wall Street Journal*. The businessman soon confides that the banking shares he bought last year now seem to be much more of a liability than an asset, and confesses that he is waiting for some world crisis—but not too big a crisis—so that he can sell off at only a small loss.

Now drinks are being served right and left, ensuring the friendly glitter of ice aloft, the warming conversations. The plane climbs safely, boldly, up through a plateau of clouds. From a cosmic perspective of course it has barely unsnuggled from earth. A few children gasp, and then whine as the unimaginable boredom of the experience takes hold;

everyone else sinks down routinely into business or pleasure. Dr. S. finally turns his attention to one of his scripts.

2

Through the very same sky that the plane sweeps, through the crowded indiscriminate atmosphere, shoot images from all directions, including several rebroadcasts of Dr. S. explaining science to everyone who cares to listen and watch. Through various regions, encabled or afloat, the discussions continue, as station after station goads the public into awareness of the latest discovery, the neatest invention.

Out of Nashville, Dr. S. is explaining the heart's magnetism, the powerful field around that organ, complete with diagrams, animations, colour simulations, and remarkable photography of someone's actual pumped-out life's blood. From time to time S. intervenes, or his voice-over highlights the slow-motion, running, breathing segments of people, their energies monitored, charted, and measured. (In the control room, technicians are watching the take and sipping coffee).

Out of Chicago, Dr. S. is explaining how animals

may predict earthquakes or volcanic eruptions. Here are close-up photographs of the sensors of hammerhead sharks. A flock of pigeons rising, then suddenly crashing down on a barn. A special graph comparing the auditory range of man with that of mice and bats. Spectacular footage of Mt. St. Helens, Oaxaca, Iran, and Chinese locations. As always, the faces of eager and serious scientists.

Out of Toronto, Dr. S. is talking about butterflies. Pictures abound. Numbers and commas, exclamations and question marks materialize on the shimmering wings of the insects. Bright colours concealing poison discourage some predators, and the same jewelled brilliance in certain habitats dazzles, conceals. Dr. S. and his cameras document patterns, pinpointing signs without codes.

The plane drones on—if day appears can night be far behind? It crosses weather systems, seismic zones, and the continent's wild geography. Mrs. Fox, discovering that he is a Pisces, lets S. down easily. It's really a terrible year for that sign, as she knows, but she doesn't say so. She covers up the news with encouraging hints about personal challenges, only confirming by her vagueness the distrust S. feels toward her pseudoscience. Yet since he's had more than one drink by now he accepts her rambling reports with some tolerance. The businessman, an Aries, is drawn in. She tells him to sell off his bank shares without fail. Well dressed, smoothly polished, with a touch of paunch, the man reminds S. of a cabinet minister he once interviewed.

As the flight attendant, a born-again Christian and, strangely enough, a Gemini, delivers his dinner of roast beef and lukewarm potatoes, red wine, and peach compote, she too is tempted to start up a conversation with the famous scientist whose identity she is now sure of. For years she has faithfully watched S. unfolding miracle after miracle, taking note with him of the promise of this new discovery or that, while sadly suspecting that he may have forgotten God. She is very anxious indeed to ask him about this possibility, but restrains herself, not being sure that her airline training program would encourage it.

S. watches her skilfully remove the remains of his half-eaten inedible compote. He has been trying without success to get his digital recorder working, and after the coffee and brandy, as his neighbours begin to sink down into leaden half-consciousness, he finally—although half in jest—asks her about the problem.

"It's important that I listen to these recordings

and interviews before we get to L.A.," he tells her, although of course it isn't.

Down its whole length the cabin has sunk into darkness, a few of the reading lights, private as candles, unwinking. The flight attendant takes the faulty recorder and tries it again and again, but apart from the foolish beep of the buttons there is nothing to be heard. Finally, however, she locates what sounds like something, a few wild whines and growls, and hands the recorder back with a smile that tells her famous passenger she is glad to have been of service.

As she moves quickly off, Dr. S. listens in perplexity to what ought to be his half-hour interview with a Florida scientist, the latest to become well known for his studies of dolphin behaviour. The interview has been processed in the Florida studio as a check on the video portion. All that comes over now, though, is a wild flurry of whistles and screeches, punctuated by a hissing silence.

"God, I hope the video didn't screw up too," he murmurs out loud, turning for sympathy to Mrs. Fox across the aisle.

She, however, like Mr. Neumann at his left elbow, has fallen fast asleep.

3

The plane wings on through the lingering light. They departed so late, the coast too is darkening; in the cabin dream filaments gather, then dissipate quickly. The patterns remain unsuspected, dreams interlocking in vast compilations like clusters of galaxies, of which only a few signals flicker briefly in the single mind.

Dr. S. dozes, then nods off to sleep. He dreams of a fox that turns to stone as he looks. As he reaches down to examine it a voice cries out, warning him that it may be rabid. Someone tells him then that he is on the air. He cannot speak, but pitches backward through a cloud. He falls, seemingly hundreds of feet. As he is about to smash into the ground he wakes up, feeling very cramped in the legs and more tired than before.

A circus of light far below, houses and highways in intricate patterns. But now the cabin is astir. Coffee and drinks are served. Mrs. Fox from Cincinnati chooses tea and after a little while seems to be reading the leaves. Mr. Neumann from Des Moines does a few stretches beside his seat. S., on his way to the toilet, runs into Yablonski, who nods and mumbles something incomprehensible. More lights below; the general chatter swells. S. has another try at his recordings; he is getting advice from right and left now, but nothing works. The flight attendant is even more sympathetic, but this time his compact silver toy is totally silent. S. meanwhile is finding the flight attendant rather attractive, and is determined to keep in humour despite this little technical failure. He asks her to dinner the next night at Garibaldi's, his favourite Los Angeles restaurant. She is overjoyed, realizing that she may be able to talk to him about some of the Big Questions after all.

The plane descends to the runway, perfection. Everyone is tired but happy to be delivered safely. Passengers disperse in all directions, relieved to be released from the forced intimacies of the trip. S. makes his way to his hotel, where he showers and falls asleep, leaving word he is to be awakened at nine in the morning. When, after a restless night, he drags himself up and tries his recorder, it works. He smiles, makes a few calls, and has breakfast. In the early afternoon, well fed and rested, he takes a taxi to the studio.

The studio occupies part of a brightly ornate building left over from the Hollywood of the thirties. On its facade, an overblown gang of satyrs chase a few frowzy nymphs. Inside, the recessed lighting glitters on polished brass fixtures. S. finds his way down a marbled corridor, turns into a large suite of offices, and approaches the familiar receptionist. She tells him that Mr. Allen is waiting for him in the projection room.

Allen, a short, bald man with a thick moustache, greets him warmly. Three shirt-sleeved technicians are fussing over a large bank of machinery. Computers, portable hard drives, and other necessities are scattered on the tables in front of them. Various-sized screens, all so far blank, surround the tables. S. drops his own techno-baggage beside a nest of wires. He flops in a chair. Allen hands him a cup of coffee and asks about the trip.

"Good," S. tells him succinctly, "I arrived in the early evening." He then explains about the unwilling voice recorder.

Allen shakes his head. "Sometimes the SSI fails," he suggests,"—or won't co-operate," and when S. responds with a puzzled look, he adds: "Solid State Intelligence—the dark enemy we depend on.... It's bound to finish us off!" He grins at Dr. S. "Just joking of course—I haven't lost my marbles. You remember John Lily? His idea, that. Crazy theories. Just theories. Let's take a look at the video."

He signals to one of the technicians. The man projects the sequences from his laptop. The other technicians slip away as the playback begins on the big screen.

Everything seems to be functioning nicely, sound as well as picture. S., dressed in a sports shirt and white trousers, is standing in a bright tropical setting, explaining. Shots of dolphins are intercut with shots of him strolling down a long beach. He continues his explanation, moving out on a finger of rock where the sea lashes wildly. The colour is perfect, the editing smooth and professional. The explanation ends with a dissolve to a medium shot of the scientist he has already introduced. The camera pulls back, revealing a very large tank. More close-ups of dolphins in action. The two scientists trade comments, voice-over.

"Looks good to me," Allen is saying.

Action sequence of dolphins. The voices fade out, the music comes up strong—part of *La Mer*, as suggested by S.

S. starts to turn to Allen to ask him whether the choice is too obvious. The dolphins come leaping, as if at the camera. S. stops in his seat. The dolphins leap out of the monitor, they cascade in the air as S. jumps away.

Dolphins spill through the air. They fall, sleek bodies flopping, across the floor of the studio.

S. staggers up out of his chair. Allen does not move, but looks up at him inquiringly, a slow sideways glance.

The dolphins continue to pour out of the monitor. They cover the floor of the studio, writhing and twisting in pain. It seems they are in pain, they are beaching themselves, they are dying. It seems they can no longer breathe.

S. can no longer breathe. A choking fit seizes him; he falls to the floor, flopping and twisting in pain.

Allen jumps out of his seat and reaches down awkwardly to grab Dr. S.

"What's the matter, for God's sake?" He shakes him, then stops suddenly. "Are you OK?"

S. rolls and writhes, helplessly scratching at sand. The sea is far away.

The technician steps forward and kills the playback. Allen is helping S. to a chair.

"Should we get a doctor?" he asks. "What the hell happened to you? Are you having a heart attack?"

S. feels himself pushed down into a chair. He stares around for a moment, blind.

"What the hell happened to you?" Allen asks again.

S. comes back to the room. He opens his eyes in surprise, and for once he is speechless. Finally, he murmurs something about jet lag, determined to get away as quickly as he can. He can see that Allen is not reassured, but there is nothing he can do. For a few minutes he just sits there, breathing heavily. As he painfully gathers his notebooks and struggles out of the studio, he can see the technicians looking at him. Something sharp and blank in their gaze makes him think of the fox.

He taxis back to the hotel and goes straight to his room, where he lies down on the bed without undressing. He stares at the ceiling for a while, then he closes his eyes. He does not sleep, but a little later feels the need to talk to a colleague. John Lilly is dead, so he thinks of Carl Sagan, then remembers that he too has passed on. He tries to contact David Suzuki, who is even then being interviewed by *People* magazine. He calls Allen and tells him that he plans to take a few days' rest. He calls the flight attendant and tells her he cannot meet her for dinner. He hangs up the phone, knowing full well he will stay in the room for some time. He lies down on the bed. It grows darker as he lies there. He does not turn on the television.

Pygmalion

Another sending. Harmon bent close to the screen. Blue lights flickered; numbers appeared; the diagram of a human body; red arrows and indicators.

He looked around, took note of the hushed empty lab, gazed at the electronic display on the wall opposite. Graphs and charts appeared there, a map showing groups of clients, scrambled light. Now, as always, the machines barely whispered; images appeared, tiny bells sounded, the printers made up charts.

Harmon was on midnight duty, alone except for the monitoring cameras. But he had long ago learned how to elude them, to mask his emotions; he had become expert at disguising the uneasiness he felt at the messages that poured in to Life Central. The lab, the whole operation, was so efficient, so remote from the messiness of the merely human.

But Harmon knew.

Somewhere in the world a man or a woman had been drinking tea, listening to music, smoking dope, having sex, reading a report, getting on a transport copter. Someone had been just waking up, going to sleep, counting profits, or calculating losses. Then it happened.

A group of cells passed the boundary of somatic lawfulness and balance, and revolted; a chemical intrusion from childhood suddenly became active; an organ, pushed to the limit, threatened to give out. A genetic imbalance began to show itself; an infection took hold in the lungs or the liver; the blood began to thin, or to thicken with poisons.

It was a beginning, a sign, a clear warning, though not yet noticed, even by the pain-transmitting system of the subject's body. It was a moment such as had been projected in the mythical flight of Zeno's arrow, a microsecond of immeasurable transition between "then" and "now," seemingly nothing, seemingly nowhere, yet fraught with significance for the person who had endured it without even experiencing it.

And just then, thanks to a tiny implanted transmitter, an enormously complex bit of machinery on which the Life Central Corporation held every kind of patent, signals would be flying back to the main monitoring station, to the company's giant computer, so large that it extended several levels below the surface of the city.

Within hours, a complete investigation would be conducted, the subject directed to a local examining unit where everything would be discovered. Treatment would be initiated at the earliest possible moment, only days, sometimes even hours, after the dysfunction had been identified. And this, despite many failures, raised the cure rate to a higher point than it had ever been in history, so high that it was almost possible to speak of a series of miracles.

Which was why the Life Central Corporation had grown to be one of the most powerful companies in the world. After all, practically nobody wanted to die if he or she didn't have to, if he or she had the money to prevent it.... New signals flashed and declared themselves: 99785-GH11L-425KH. Harmon's fingers moved quickly across the keyboard. Yes, he was onto it now, beginning to get a sense of the subject's body, feeling his way into his blood and bone. (It was a male, forty years old, a Caucasian, with a long history of good health, though there was a disturbing record of stress, occasional breakdowns, possibly drug-related.)

As he probed further and began his detailed readout, Harmon noticed certain telltale signs, the most prominent of which was a slight interference with the signal transmission between the subject's nerves and the brain. That was probably what had triggered off the Life Central alarm system. After several thousand probes, conducted at rapid speed, using the microchips implanted near the subject's brain stem, Harmon eliminated many possibilities. He took a scan of the nerve network, and noticed an amazing fact: there was scar tissue in several places along the subject's myelin sheathing: somehow, the soft, white, fatty substance that surrounds the nerves had been damaged.

MS-35, he thought at once, *the contemporary mutation of a nineteenth-century disease. Dysfunction resulting from blocked paths in the nervous system, due to myelin scarring.*

Quickly he typed out his report: *Life Central 44793 to Code 997GH. Immediate probe suggested: CAT scan, MRI, PGL. Urgent. Symptom watch mandatory: sensory, ataxia, paresis, optic, diplopia, vertigo, dysarthria, facial numbness, bladder difficulties, Lhermitte's sign, facial palsy, trigeminal neuralgia, headache, nausea, vomiting, etc., etc.*

But even as he made up his report, as his brain calculated and his agile fingers moved, Harmon felt it coming on, some vague disturbance in himself, something without a name, but palpable, a soul-sickness, a malaise no longer recognized by science, or else diminished and discounted every day by mere analysis and measurement.

He drew back, his sweating fingers hovering nervously over the keyboard. A numbness had crept suddenly into his left leg—not just "pins and needles," but a feeling of dead weight at the bone. At the same time, the screens in front of him had suddenly begun to blur and flicker, and he felt a tingling in his neck and left shoulder.

Harmon struggled for control, for mastery of his own body. He slipped out of his comfortable chair and stood shivering, terrified, in front of the battery of equipment. He stared hopelessly at the multi-dimensional blueprints, at the screens full of numbers.

Desperately, he resisted the onset, the attack; he tried to ignore the symptoms. But it was no good, the symptoms were undeniable. Once again he had begun to imagine himself into the body of his subject;

once again he was suffering the dysfunctions he had predicted for that unknown person, and once again he had the eerie feeling that the machinery had somehow "tainted" him, that the experience of a subject thousands of miles distant had thrust on him physical manifestations that the unknown victim himself had not even experienced yet.

Harmon closed his eyes. *I've got to fight it off,* he told himself, *to pretend that nothing's happening. They'll see me, they'll know. They mustn't know—*

Someone laid a hand on his shoulder.

2

He woke up in the familiar space of his company apartment. He felt calm and almost rested; he could move his arms and legs, and he had no difficulty getting up. His memory seemed clear and strong.

What he remembered, though, came in fragments. Immediately after his breakdown, the managers, Palmer and Tanaka—sympathetic and unflappable, as usual—had questioned him in the pleasant confines of the company lounge. They had hardly raised their voices: two fine gentlemen, relaxed and fit in their expensive shirts and jeans, smiling at him and from time to time offering him herbal tea and organic biscuits.

He had been taken ill at his post, they reminded him, an unfortunate seizure due to nervous strain—nothing serious. They referred to his file, to reports of his fellow-workers, then conferred quietly with each other. They told him that his case would be examined as soon as the next Personnel Board met. Meanwhile, he would be relieved of his duties—with full pay and pension benefits, of course. Their only caution was that he not leave his housing unit until his case could be dealt with.

"I don't have to remind you of the security problem," Palmer explained. "We have evidence of strong corporate guerrilla activity in the area. We wouldn't want you to be victimized by one of the gangs that seem to be monitoring headquarters here. You have a nice long retirement to look forward to...."

Harmon was well aware that Life Central serviced mostly the rich and powerful, who benefited wonderfully from the early diagnosis and enjoyed the highest cure rate known in human history. Ordinary people, of course, had to wait for the usual symptoms. Since huge profits were being made, and governments could be overturned if health information was leaked, only a few high executives of the firm had access to the real names of the clients. Industrial sabotage was rampant. In the past, technicians like Harmon had been kidnapped, brainwashed to obtain information, and then killed. For that reason Life Central insisted that its employees live within special compounds, where they could be protected and watched, and then, later, retired to Elysian surroundings—company pleasure parks—with their memories purged.

To join Life Central was to enlist for the duration; to be forced to serve until a "phase-out" date, when you were gradually taken away from your area of expertise, "de-briefed" into innocence, and returned to a society you barely knew but were encouraged to luxuriate in, a society of beautiful similitudes and carefully programmed stage settings. Out there, thanks to technology and the company's expertise, you enjoyed all the pleasures of flesh and spirit that clever men could provide for you. Not surprisingly, when word filtered back from those who had been "released," they said their new life was bliss; all the dreary years behind them had been well worth it....

Harmon lay for a while on his large sofa and thought things over. He had a strong sense that the company would ask him to retire. If he was right, his career was finished, fifteen years short of the scheduled date. It was a shock, and he was surprised to find that he had almost been expecting it—that he almost welcomed it. If they were going to sever him it would mean a cut in retirement pay, but they would take care of him, he knew that.

He climbed to his feet and began pacing up and down the room, trying to imagine what it would be like to be free.

He realized at that moment that he had come to take for granted the dreary routines of his existence. He thought of all the lonely breakfasts eaten to piped-in music and vidnetworks; of communal lunches and "meditations," or "exercises," with his fellow employees, known only by their numbers; of evenings spent with his company-assigned "drone," a street girl taken from one of the shack cities that surrounded the capital and specially programmed for pleasure skills.

No more night watches in front of flashing screens; no more miraculous probes, or rescue missions. No more empathy with distant bodies tagged only with number codes. He could walk clear of the compound, escape the dreary city. He could live in a pleasure park, where a bountiful life would be provided.

In the first shock of his awareness that his life was changing he felt burdened, and almost regretful.

It would be difficult, starting all over. But then he remembered his treasures....

He got up, crossed the room quickly, and pressed a button. Doors opened and he walked down a long hall decorated with astrological emblems and signs—the figures of constellations, scenes from classical mythology. It was this walk, performed daily, that had first given him the idea.

Just a few steps and he came to a door with the familiar number 77. He punched in a code: panels rolled noiselessly back, lights flashed on, and Harmon entered his own private living space.

A soft robotic voice bade him welcome. He looked around and saw that everything was in order, perfect as usual—the appliances and contoured chairs, the adjustable metal tables, the convenient vidscreens, the sleeping space—all bathed in the soothing colours of the recessed lights.

Harmon went straight to the familiar panel that gave access to his inner storage space, pushed a button, and, as the doors slid back and the lights came up, beheld his collection. He stood back smiling, almost overcome with joy at the sight of his treasures.

Yes, he thought, *my companions*, collected with infinite patience and resource over a whole decade, magnificent objects hidden away behind the videos and tapes, the billiard table, the antique clothing, foot-gear and hats that filled the room up to its bright metal ceiling.

As always, this first sight of them took his breath away. They were so like living presences—and yet.... Harmon stared at them, forgetting everything else in the sheer rapture of contact and possession. He stepped close enough to take in every lovingly remembered detail, close enough to touch them. He walked among them, his fingers ran across the curves and bulges of the marble, he touched the cool sweating bronze.

They dazzled him, as always, and in his mind he greeted them, almost ritually, each in its turn.

There stood the youthful Hermes, the magician god, the messenger, with his smiling inward gaze. And on his shoulder, the infant Dionysus, young god of ecstasy and wine. (He'd traded a great deal of leave-time for the tip that led him to that wondrous pair.) And there was glorious Aphrodite, stepping out of her drapery like a dream of pleasure. (She had come to him through a street girl, who sold the image for a pittance to buy herself a new outfit.)

Beside her, Athena, the serene one, patroness of learning, with her gaze reaching deep into human consciousness (a gift from a dying professor of cognitive science who had admired Harmon's taste and enthusiasm).

And, finally, Zeus, father of gods and men, in gleaming bronze, with pointed beard and arms outstretched, about to hurl his thunderbolt across time and space. (Harmon had won this piece in a lottery; a few of his colleagues had consoled him for having to settle for such a piece of junk, when there were valuable things to be won—trips to the planetary colonies, class-A drone girls....)

Harmon fetched himself a drink and sat down before his treasures. As always, he remained only slightly aware of their deficiencies. The hand of Hermes—it must have once held the god's magic wand, the caduceus—was broken off. Aphrodite's nose was smashed and flat. Athena's owl was but a fragment on her shoulder. Zeus's great metallic thunderbolt, once grasped in his strong, shining fingers, had vanished.

These faults were nothing to Harmon. Quite the contrary, they only served to enhance, as he thought, the dignity and power of the figures—timeless bodies wrought in marble and bright metal, but also touched by time and trouble, and all the more human for that. Wonderful figures,

Harmon knew, bringing order and dignity to the space they inhabited. Their presence turned his tiny living space into something like a temple.

At first he'd been amazed that almost no one else appeared to be interested in the statues. Was it because they seemed unworthy of the body image fostered by Life Central? Because they failed to measure up to the standards of perfection proclaimed by the utilitarian civilization of the present day? Or perhaps the sheer passage of time, and new mythologies, had sunk the old Greek pantheon into oblivion, as in a famous story by the German poet Heine.

Harmon's education, of course, had virtually ignored both the literary classics and history. He was a technician, and only a few of the elite were trained or informed beyond their required instrumental knowledge. The study of the Humanities was not encouraged. It was assumed that such study posed a distinct threat to the social order. But in this case Harmon didn't need formal training; his intuition told him everything. The statues had been a revelation. He saw at once that the ancient artists had rendered the human body in its true perfection, in its full grace and blessedness. Despite the missing limbs, the cracked and broken features, the tiny flaws and faults in the marble, those artists had caught, with a rare power, a clear vision of humanity, whole and radiant. And Harmon had loved them from the first.

Yet now, in the midst of his pleasure, he stepped back. The sad thought came to him that with a reduced income, on a pension, he could afford no more such purchases. Money was scarcer than ever, he couldn't save, and perhaps when he moved to the pleasure parks his contact with the bleak cities, where there might be more lost treasures, would be cut off forever.

If that were the case, if the company prevented him from exploring for more statues, he knew he would spend his retirement working to learn more about the ones he already possessed. Already he had acquired books full of valuable information, and a few electronic files—and of course he could read more in the park libraries. He would make his new home a haven for those who felt as he did. New friends would gather round him; perhaps he could share his excitement about his collection at last....

At that moment the bell of his flat announced a visitor.

He pressed the mechanism, carefully shutting up his collection, vidscreened the new arrival, and, when he saw who it was, cautiously opened the door.

Minutes later he was pouring tea for Palmer and Tanaka and listening to their reasonable explanation of the process that would lead to his retirement.

3

Sunlight flooded the hospital room.

Harmon woke as from a long dream. He stared at the tidy bed, the attractive furnishings, but his glance was drawn inexorably through the room's tall double windows.

A green lawn stretched away toward a tall grove of poplars. He saw benches, flowerbeds of dazzling yellow roses. A robin sang in the branch of an old maple tree, squirrels dashed toward the gnarled trunks. The blue sky arched over everything.

This sight, after so many years in the artificiality of the compound, moved Harmon almost to tears. But he sobbed quietly to himself, hoping that the thin young nurse of his fevered recollection would not come and chastise him in her no-nonsense way.

After a while, he grew used to the dazzling scene.

He knew that the company had created the image of the garden just for him. It was a virtual reality projection, based on what they imagined he might respond to. Even so, something was missing—his most secret life, something they would hardly understand.

He realized they had washed clear his mind of the Life Central formulas, that all his skills, acquired over the years, had been obliterated. It was a relief.

He smiled, dozed, fell into a dream. When he woke up, a small woman with short curly white hair and round cherubic cheeks sat in the chair beside his bed.

"I'm Dr. Larkin," she explained, "your counsellor." She shook his hand firmly. "You know, you look great! They've really achieved perfection with you, Mr. Harmon."

He barely heard her. There was something he was attempting to remember, but it hung on the edge of his mind for mere seconds, then disappeared, a shadow devoured by a deeper shadow.

"I'm told you were the best programmer they ever had. Really put yourself into your work. No one to match you for diagnosis. And now you're looking just wonderful—and with your whole life ahead of you!"

For a second Harmon thought she might shake his hand again.

"It's easy to see that they've given you the complete treatment. Mr. Tanaka was just telling me they've never done such a thing before. But in your case they felt it was only fair compensation—because you've had to retire a little early, I mean."

"The complete treatment...?"

It was maddening; she insisted on talking, and he was so hard pressed to remember.

"Surely you know what I mean? They've used the full resources of Life Central to give you the ultimate health scan and refurbishing. They've done it all: the plastic surgery, the muscle remoulding. Wonderfully creative and natural. Why don't you just have a look?"

She went to the table and brought back a small hand mirror and gave it to him. He lifted it slowly, and gasped.

He did look wonderful—much younger, more handsome, yet completely recognizable, himself. He became aware suddenly of how strong he felt, with what supple ease his body moved.

"You've got a terrific life ahead of you, Mr. Harmon," she told him. "And the pleasure parks are all open to you now. You can forget the gloomy old past; those compound flats aren't so inspiring, are they?"

Something turned over in Harmon's mind. He

reached down and held the sides of the bed with his hands.

Doctor Larkin stared at him. "What on earth's the matter? You look so odd all of a sudden."

"*My flat—all the things in my flat!*" he whispered. Memories were flooding back. They had explained it all so patiently. Then, when he had protested, they had used the drugs. Now he couldn't get any more words out.

"Well, you know what they have to do." Dr. Larkin had taken over the hand mirror and was brushing at her front curls. "It's the regulations. Nothing to be removed from the compound—too much risk of smuggling out company secrets. Everything destroyed and recycled. To be replaced in due course. A clean new life. And for you, Mr. Harmon, practically a new body. You'll be the envy of every Life Central programmer. God! I wish they'd give me a makeover like yours!"

She almost winked, nudging him gently through the coverlets.

Harmon fell back on his pillow.

"Go away," he whispered fiercely. "Please...go away."

He closed his eyes; he would not look at her, at the room, at the false reality of the garden outside....

But he heard her voice again, heard her stirring in her chair.

"Ah, well, a little relapse.... But I'll be back. I'll do all I can to help. You must rest now—and not worry about anything, Mr. Harmon."

He listened as she left the room, still refusing to open his eyes. Instead, he bent his concentration inward. He saw the statues, held them in his vision: the imperishable ones. There stood all-knowing Zeus, ruler of gods and men, with his powerful arms and his eagle-like gaze; tender Aphrodite ready to embrace the world; sly Hermes hoisting up Dionysus, child seer of the ancient mysteries. And noble Athena, wise and virtuous.... They were gone now, gone forever. He knew the company would make no mistakes, would tolerate no exceptions, no sentimental attachments.

Harmon's deepest, truest contact with his past was broken. And his thoughts, his dreams, his memories, also broken, drifted aimlessly now through his numbed mind....

He opened his eyes slowly. He gazed around the sunlit room, aware of the powerful vitality of his body, feeling the strength in his arms, the surge of energy in his chest and loins.

He climbed from the bed, stripped off his white

gown and stood naked before the full-length wall mirror. For a moment or two he simply stared, stunned and taken aback. He was suddenly shy, almost frightened by his own body, by the image that stared back at him from the mirror—but he caught his breath, swallowed, and continued to look.

He took in the broad, strong shoulders, the powerful chest and arms, moulded to a muscular perfection. He was dazzled by the thick, dark, lustrous hair, by the soft glowing beauty of the skin. He looked much taller, both sharp-eyed and strong. Could it be? Could this really be *Harmon*, the man he was inwardly conscious of, moment by moment? Could this be his true self?

Yes, yes, there he was—strong enough, lithe enough, to wrestle with some god, or to spring naked upon the back of a magnificent stallion. Their technology has done it for him; they had given him the body of a hero. He himself has become an Apollo, a youthful and muscular god, and a life of unimagined pleasure lay before him in the new Elysium of the company's retirement parks.

He groaned. A wave of disgust overcame him. It was all a deceit and a nightmare! They had changed him, moulded him as they pleased. They'd cheated him, abused him by making him beautiful.

No, he didn't want it—the company's gift of youth and beauty.

The statues were gone, the ancient ones, and he missed them. His soul longed for them, and he realized now, more than ever, that he'd loved them, not because they embodied power and beauty, but because of their very imperfections.

He knew that he had grown to treasure the human pathos of those cracked torsos and broken limbs, which nonetheless gave a hint of something higher. He knew that he had come to love them, not as gods and goddesses, all-powerful and remote, but as companions, themselves battered and broken by their journey through time.

But now they were gone forever.

He groaned, and with one motion tore the lamp from his bedside table and flung it at the mirror, at his own transformed image. A crash and the tinkle of glass was followed by silence, then voices and quick footsteps sounding in the hall outside.

But he didn't care; nothing mattered to him now, and he stood there trembling, listening without hope to his own strong heartbeats, enduring every hateful breath.

Sargon and the Fabulous Guests

The mother has forgotten her new child, who once, in a moment of blinding pain, rescued her from the terror of light and touch. That was a while ago, the birth. The forgetting happened slowly.

The hospital is the first place to mention, white and fairly clean. It was in an old section of the city, a worn brick building that they had trouble getting into because it was 2:00 a.m. Even though the forms were filled out and the insurance applied for, the door was locked to them—to the mother, the father, and the father's mother. When they finally got in, they waited while the forms were typed. The father, slightly nervous, pointed to the floor, where a few insects scurried. His mother shook her head;

it really wasn't very clean. The wife was too busy with her pain to notice.

Finally, they got to the right ward. The case room was quiet, expectancies toned to a dull somnolence by the epidurals. It was like a church at night, with lights burning, except in the waiting room, which was like a bus station. In there the smoke rolled fiercely out of the teeth of four Natives, smoking against the rules, and the improvised ashtrays spilled butts. It was butts the Natives talked of, too, the butts, bums, bottoms of all their previous children. This one would have a bum too, but not be one, with any luck. Laughter and smoke.

So the father and his mother left the woman there, in the ward, and didn't wait, because of the Natives. It was a long lying-in, and they returned many times during the next days until the baby was born.

The boy came quietly, in dimmed light, to the mother's eye. For a moment she saw him with clear and perfect sharpness. The doctor and the midwife congratulated her. He was taken away to be weighed and was called Richard.

After the great effort of the birth, the mother fell sick. It was her blood, they said, the doctor had to order transfusions.

She fed the baby from her breasts. It was her first baby and she was surprised that it was so light. They put her in a room with the wife of a famous football player, and the nurses said her baby was too light. The baby of the football player's wife was heavier. Its head was covered by a thin mesh of tangled black curls. Strangely enough, it had a smaller penis than her baby did.

Richard had very strange eyes. At first they seemed blue, light blue, but when you looked more closely the left eye showed traces of mottled yellow. From certain angles, the iris seemed to glow with pink or yellow light.

After the first day the mother felt that her baby knew her, and she wondered when he would know his name. She understood very little about babies, but it pleased her to call him names from the book she had bought, from which she had already chosen his real name. Some of the names were lovely: Sargon, Moses, Karna, Paris, Cyrus. But now he had his own name, so it was no good thinking of that. It was better to look at the dozen roses her husband had sent, at the rush basket in which the fruit from his mother lay all bright and glassy—though it was real fruit.

(The football player and his wife had named their baby Jason.)

The mother's sickness kept her in the hospital for some extra days. The football player came to take his wife home, laughing and joking with the nurses. The mother was well enough to read movie magazines. She read about Johnny Depp, Nicole Kidman, and Angelina Jolie, about Robert Mitchum, Franchot Tone, Mary Pickford, and Rudolf Valentino. Some of them were having problems, others were dying or dead, or being remembered, or forgotten. It was all in the pictures, she really didn't have to read it. It passed the time.

Finally, she could go home. They lived in a tiny second-floor apartment on the other side of the city from the hospital. It was an old house divided into many units so that the landlord could rent all the available space. Though they occupied the second floor, it was dark, because most of the windows faced on an alley. From her kitchen the woman could see into the living room and bedroom, though sometimes, when the husband was practising he would go into the bedroom and shut the door. Then she could not see, but she could hear the falsely struck guitar chords as he built up the music to a genuine tune. He had bought the guitar in the sixties, when he was living in a commune, but had not played it for a long time. Now he would practise again, while she preferred to watch television.

It made a curious counterpoint, because she watched all the talk shows, day and night, and he would go into the bedroom to practise. So Oprah would be talking to Deepak Chopra, Jon Stewart to Michelle Obama, Charlie Rose to Henry Kissinger, Johnny Carson to Jane Fonda, or Dick Cavett to Philip Roth, and music would begin, hesitant and frail, and in the back of her mind she would wait for the flub, which would come very soon, whether the tune was "The Times They Are a-Changin'" or "Buttercup Girl."

During the day, of course, it was better, because he worked in the post office supervising one of the machines that sorted the mail, and he seldom got home before five-thirty and there were no big shows then.

For the baby, his mother had given them a crib, which they put in the living room. It was one you could plug in and it would make a gentle rocking motion, so the baby would seldom cry, even when she was slow to get up to feed him. She would sometimes get up, especially during the first weeks, push the wall-plug that turned on both the television and the rocking mechanism of the crib, and make coffee. She sat drinking coffee until she was awake, which at some point happened, and then she would take the baby and feed him. He was a very quiet baby at first, hardly looking out of his crib at all, but later he seemed to get restless.

She would be watching a rerun of the Dick Cavett Show and drinking coffee in the afternoon and the baby would start to cry. So she would plug in the crib and sit watching the stray beams of sunshine from somewhere reflected oddly on his mismatched eyes. Then he would suddenly turn his head as if something had passed by, but of course there was nothing. She thought it was the change of light patterns when they switched to and from the commercials.

Naturally, she was quite weak after her sickness, and sometimes she would go through the whole day and not even get dressed, never mind try to go out. Occasionally in the bathroom she would stand on the scales naked and try to see herself in the small mirror, but could only get a twisted craning version of her body, which she knew had gone badly flabby in several places. Or she would sit rubbing her folded out belly, staring at the strange lines and crinkles, which might have been a map for a country that she had dreamed about but not visited.

But mostly his mother would come and they would sit drinking coffee in silence, watching the talk shows on which the fabulous guests strutted out, one by one, and listening to all the interesting talk about the problems of being famous and successful. She would think how wonderful it must be to find so many words and so much humour to deal with all those problems, to be so entertaining, and not to mind moving over when the next guest appeared.

As she sat there, usually she followed everything, but sometimes, especially when her husband would be trying to play the guitar in the next room, her mind sailed off she didn't know where, and she would catch herself thinking of the hospital, or about herself as a little girl, or even about her new baby and why it was born with no hair.

One thing she thought of often was the time when she was a little girl and visited the bottling factory in her town with the fourth-grade class. It was a very large milk-bottling factory, the kind they had in those days, a big bruised building that sprawled around the railroad tracks and sent up great plumes of smoke from its high brick chimney. She remembered the trucks and the big entranceway and the conveyors that wound through the buildings like shining silver guts. And the bottles, all clear and gleaming, that jiggled along the conveyor in an endless row, only to come rattling out of the filler so perfectly white. It fascinated her because of how it went on, that conveyor, and because of the comical, busy look of the bottles, which seemed to be circling always between full and empty, but one of them she knew would be on her doorstep in the morning, so she had some idea of the part she played in it.

But of course she almost never thought of her life in the past now. She was too busy just keeping up with all the exciting new faces of the present day; she was too busy taking care of her baby that still often cried in the night. And one day when her husband came home early he found her staring openmouthed at all the baby's clothes that she still had to wash, and wondering what to do for dinner. What he didn't know was that she couldn't jump up and do anything right then because she was thinking of that trip to the bottle factory, which had suddenly come into her mind as soon as she pressed the button to turn off the TV, God knows why.

Her husband looked at her and said nothing. She heard him getting a beer from the fridge, and heard him go into the bedroom. He came out with his guitar, set his beer on the table, and began tuning the instrument. He didn't look at the baby, of course, because the baby was obviously fine.

He played a bit of "Oh! Susannah," but soon struck a few really false notes. He put the guitar down carefully and came over to where she sat, and crouching down in front of her, his face contorted with a strange kind of elusive pain, said, "What's your name? Please tell me your name."

She noticed that he had very deep brown eyes, like hers, and wondered about her baby's blue ones. She could not think of her name when she was asked just like that. "I'm not sure," she said numbly.

"You know it's Merle," he said.

"Yes."

He turned away in a fit of uneasy laughter, which frightened her. She got up to take care of the baby's clothes, and saw her husband disappear into the bedroom. In a little while the guitar noises came from there but she couldn't recognize any tune.

That night the baby began to cry. It wouldn't stop crying when she fed it and changed it, so she gave it some gripe water and rocked it for a while on her knee, but when she tried to put it back in the crib it started to cry again. Even the mechanical rocker didn't seem to help, and she began to worry about it.

"Richard," she asked the baby, "what's the matter with you?"

Finally, the baby went to sleep with her on the sofa. Her husband didn't wake up at all during this. Dimly, she was aware of him leaving for work in the morning. She was very tired.

Just before noon the baby began to cry again and wouldn't stop unless she held him continuously.

So she called the doctor, and when she couldn't reach him she spoke to the nurse about it.

"How old is the baby?" the nurse asked in a distant, official voice.

"Nearly four months."

"You have a colicky baby, most likely. Or else he's starting to teethe in a big way. The doctor will prescribe some Tempra drops. He'll call you as soon as he has a free moment."

By late afternoon he had not called, but the baby had stopped crying. It was another afternoon of reruns, but these she had never seen. One of the guests fascinated her so much that she sank down into her chair and forgot the baby, her husband, the doctor, and even that she was watching and not overhearing a conversation.

It was a man from a child agency who was telling Oprah about the black market babies. It seemed there was a lively trade in unwanted babies, that you could get a great deal of money for a healthy white baby, because of the difficulty with official adoption. The conversation went on and on, and she listened open-mouthed.

The phone rang shortly afterward but she paid no attention. She let it ring and ring until it stopped. Her husband came home and the television ran on. By this time they had reached Sesame Street, or the Friendly Giant, or Kukla, Fran and Ollie, which she never watched.

She heard her husband storming around in the kitchen, but she said nothing at all, not even when he sank down on the sofa and drank off three beers with a quick, furtive motion. A little later he went out, slamming the door.

It was very late and she was all but asleep when he came back that night, clumsy and crashing, past the sofa and into the bedroom. In the morning he left early.

After he had gone she got up very quietly to get her coffee, but as she moved across the room, watching the baby all the while, she stepped against an object that made her stop short and almost lose her balance. He had set the guitar against the coffee table and she hadn't even noticed. Slowly it sank to the floor, looking like a funny shrunken coat rack, making a hollow kind of plunk as it settled. She stepped around it gingerly to pick it up, and the baby began to cry, softly at first, as if it were crying inward into some dream, then louder as she stood there wringing her hands in helpless frustration.

Now she had no medicine for the baby because the doctor hadn't called or she hadn't answered, her husband was angry because she couldn't always remember her name, and her mother-in-law had gone to Florida. She hushed the baby as best she could, drinking cup after cup of coffee, not even turning on the morning shows until she had made up her mind and actually begun to dress him, and herself, to meet the cold morning air.

Outside, the streets were almost empty. A few cars stirred and coughed into motion, sliding out from hidden driveways. She walked up to where the bus stop was, opposite the neighbourhood grocery, happy about the nice fresh pink that was creeping into her baby's cheeks, thinking how sly he looked with that strong searching glance buried deeply in those strange blue eyes. Then the bus came, roaring and groaning around the corner, a desolate bauble with all its lights set against the flat grey gloom of the morning.

It was the first time she had taken her baby on a bus, and he seemed to like the motion, because he smiled up at her suddenly, almost his first real smile, and an old woman sitting opposite leaned over and began to fuss over him, asking how old he was, if he was a boy, what his name was, and so on interminably—until they were almost downtown and the bus began to fill up and she had to shut up.

Well, it was too bad if he had decided now that he was going to be good, the mother thought. It would all end the minute they got home. He would start to cry and nobody would ever sleep and her husband would blame her and nothing would ever be right. She looked down at her little boy, who had dozed off, and felt a very soft slow-moving pressure as of a very gently warm fingertip run down her right cheek. But it was only a tear.

She got out where she thought would be best, near the market, and hurried between the shabby, faceless buildings, in which some old and forgotten machinery seemed to be running on to such purposes as she could hardly imagine. The market square itself she barely recognized, though she had been there many times before. Trucks and vans everywhere in motion, piled-up boxes concealing the glassy storefronts, little swirls of furious activity, and shouts in many strange languages reverberating under the dim arcade.

This was the place, she thought (where else?), but at first she didn't really know what to do next, so she wandered among the stalls that were being set up and watched the produce being unboxed—a spilling out of eggs and oranges, cauliflower, carrots, apples, and bananas, making little inert splashes of colour on the tables at which there were still very few buyers. Finally, she got up courage to ask one red-faced man in overalls about what she had come for, but he turned on her with a huge shrug and babbled something in a foreign language, his hands and jaws working in furious rhythms that she couldn't read. Another man came over and she tried to make him understand, but he stood there, motionless and blank, as if he regretted a little the secret joke that was lost between them. She started then to move away, feeling altogether heavy and helpless, when a third man appeared, who seemed to have overheard, and who understood. He began to say something, sputtering and angry, then changed his mind and pointed sharply behind her, as if he were ordering her to clear out altogether.

Turning, though, she saw a narrow alley leading into the main market building, to which he might have been directing her, and she gladly went where he seemed to be pointing, afraid of making a scene over the whole business.

Inside, she walked in a glare of light between rows of shut-up boutiques, the windows reflecting in duplicate soaring ghosts that brushed across brilliant displays. All at once she was beginning to feel a kind of despair, seeing her child stir under her chin—yawning with closed eyes, snug in its carrying straps—but she kept on walking and came finally to a place where the corridor joined up with a larger inside mall. Here, in front of a shuttered storefront, sat an old woman, bent over a table on which were placed dozens of antique glass bottles of various sizes.

Hesitating, she looked first at the woman, who was wrapped in a shawl and might have been asleep, and then up and down the length of the corridor. It was cavernous and almost empty, though at one end an old man was vigorously sweeping, and at the other someone she couldn't see seemed to be hammering on a kind of metal.

Suddenly she realized that the woman's head had moved and that she was looking up at her with very dark, greedy, anxious eyes.

"So you've come to sell your baby?" the woman said in a flat indifferent voice, her gums rolling pink as she spoke, her shawl drawn tighter around her by a pair of scrawny, eager arms.

She did not know what to answer, but nodded helplessly, staring down at the rows of dusty bottles, feeling the woman's gaze cut through her, afraid of what she would ask next.

The old woman said nothing more, however, but, with a long, drawn-out groan of resignation, dragged herself to her feet, steadied her bent body for a moment against the table, and then tottered away with slow staggering steps in the direction of the man who was sweeping.

It seemed to take a long time for her to reach him, and he made no effort at all to advance to meet her, though he looked up a few times as she came closer, then finally stopped sweeping altogether when she was no more than a few steps away.

There followed a long muttered exchange between them as the mother watched from a distance, clutching her baby, which moved restlessly in her arms now, perhaps because it was listening to the wild furtive beating of her heart.

After a while the old woman turned and began the slow, painful walk back. Under her arm she carried what looked like a small white plastic bag. Down the length of the corridor the man was sweeping again, paying no attention. The distant metallic hammering continued.

She took the bag from the old woman and opened it, feeling very nervous under the scrutiny of those black, beady eyes. Inside was a frayed, worn-looking roll of bills, held together by a rubber band. Idly, almost dreamily, the mother fingered the bills. She was aware of the old woman's eager eyes on her. The bills numbered twenty, each in the denomination of a thousand dollars.

She started to say something, then changed her mind. She shoved the packet of bills into her coat pocket. The bag fluttered down to the polished floor.

Fumbling a little with the straps, she finally untangled her baby. Richard looked up at her with a calm, uninquisitive gaze. She passed him over to the old woman, turned, and ran in sheer terror back down the corridor.

Outside, the market square seemed suddenly crowded, as if she had been away for a long time. She thought she saw the three men she had asked for directions standing over a huge barrow of apples, pointing at her and whispering together.

She kept on running for nearly the length of the block, then slowed down, out of breath, and hastily shoved the empty carrying straps inside her coat. Someone might think, if they saw those straps, that she had somehow carelessly lost her baby. But of course she had not lost it but sold it, because it was necessary to bring peace and to make her husband happy. All the way home on the bus she hummed a little song to herself. She felt so much lighter and happier.

When she finally shut the door behind her, the apartment seemed very dark and small. She put the coffee on right away, and just managed to catch the final segment of Dr. Phil. While she was watching, she folded up the baby's crib and got it tucked away under the bed. She threw all the baby's toys and clothes there also.

She took time making dinner, grilling a steak from the freezer, cutting up the green beans, making a soup and boiling the potatoes. As she worked, Sesame Street and the news flashed by. Her husband was very late. Perhaps he would come just before bedtime and miss dinner. This thought made her rather sad.

It grew late, and the meal, done at last, had to be held. She found herself very hungry, wondering where he might be, and she began to nibble a little at the food. She ate more and more, and soon she had finished nearly everything. She took one of his bottles of beer from the fridge and drank it slowly, but still there was no sign of him. She made coffee and flipped over to the news and watched the news reel itself out, item by item: world news, local news, sports, then finally the weather. He did not come. She picked up his guitar and strummed it idly, discordantly. Finally, she opened another beer and swallowed it quickly, together with a handful of pills.

She slept, then woke up feeling very ill. There was no sign of him. The television continued to unfold the news in bright little snippets, the newsreader smiling all the while, and the world's troubles interspersed with clever little ads. It went on and on, the same stories returning, sometimes a little changed. The shifts were imperceptible. She understood nothing of it. She tried to sleep some more.

He did not come back that day, nor the next. She lay on the sofa, thinking of nothing, sometimes changing the stations. She watched even the fabulous guests from a great distance of hunger and pain. All their talk, all their wonderful sentences, rolled on her eardrums, like strange voices she had heard as a child on the edge of sleep, almost soothing. Their smiles touched her brow like feathers. She got up and stood in the kitchen, chewing on a few stale slices of bread, then lay on the sofa for a long time staring at the ceiling.

On the third day, when a vision of her child crept slowly back into her mind and she thought that she might just get up and make sure of the money, her husband returned. He arrived before dinner time and, edging into the room with a nervous smile, he pulled the door closed, his hands behind him on the doorknob, hidden. She lay there staring at him, unable to say anything. Slowly he surveyed the room, the disorder, the blaring TV, her listless form on the sofa. Then, without a word, he went into the kitchen and she heard him open and then slam the fridge door. She heard the pop of the beer-cap, and he appeared again, a beer bottle in his right fist.

"I was on a trip," he said.

"I sold the baby," she said.

The beer bottle seemed to fall slowly, so slowly she could almost read the label. It bounced on the rug and the beer gurgled out in a thin plume of froth.

He saw at once that she was telling the truth; he had missed something in the room and now he knew what it was.

He opened his mouth, and a loud howl seemed to tear him apart, yet to remain outside him, as if it had found him standing there and entered him.

He grew suddenly restless. Up and down he went,

pacing the length of the small apartment. He disappeared into the bedroom, immediately reappeared, and walked the length of the place to the kitchen. He repeated this pattern in ever quicker motions until he was almost running. At one point he stopped and picked up his guitar. He stood there, his hands striking at the strings, but it made no sense.

She brought him some of the pills. He took a handful and lay on the sofa groaning.

The next morning he would not get up, but took more of the pills, washing them down with several bottles of beer. She decided she would have to try to find the child, and drank cup after cup of coffee until she felt well enough to go out. She had slept on the floor by the foot of the sofa because she did not like to be in the bedroom alone. She explained to him what she intended to do.

Soon after, she slipped out of the apartment, the money stuffed into her coat pocket. She left the television on to cheer him up. She took a taxi straight to the market. The driver tried to make conversation but she had nothing to say and he soon ignored her. But he did tell her it was foolish to rest her head against the window, and then drove on with a kind of vicious recklessness. She paid no attention.

The market was already crowded. She had arrived

rather late. When she got to the inner arcade, the old woman was nowhere to be seen. She ran up and down in a panic, staring into each shop in turn. Many were still shut up tight, but in others, salespeople behind locked doors prepared for the coming day, flitting about between the counters like animated manikins. After a while she was exhausted and collapsed onto a bench among some stringy half-withered plants. In despair she leaned back, shutting her eyes.

When she opened them, she saw, through an angle of yellow leaves, the old man sweeping. She recognized him at once and ran to him. Her words poured out, a little too loudly, across the arcade. A few people turned to stare and smile. The old man listened impassively, resting on his broom, staring at her intently with his sharp little eyes.

He said at last that there might be something that could be done about it. She should make up her mind though, he said. He could promise nothing at all, but she should come back tomorrow, much earlier. He would see what he could do.

She went home wearily, with slow heavy steps. She could not bear to take the bus, to be shut up in a taxi. She moved at last with a growing fury through the alien streets.

When she got home, her husband was better, sitting on the couch, drinking coffee. He listened to her in silence, his eyes shining with a brilliant blankness. He said they could not call the police, for fear of trouble. He himself would go in the morning. He would do what he could, he said in a sinking voice.

They sat up all night, drinking coffee. From time to time, he strummed his guitar, fitting new music to some words that she didn't understand, making many mistakes but going always further until the song was finished.

At the first sign of daybreak he left without a word.

She waited all day in a frenzy of nervous terror. She wanted to set up the crib but could not bear to touch it, or the toys, or any of the baby's clothes.

All day she listened for his steps on the stairs, moving back and forth between the door and the window, only sometimes stopping to let the images from the television take hold of her. She wanted those colours to wash over her, to dissolve her into themselves, all those reds and yellows and blues flickering there as she fixed on them with an ever tighter, ever more vicious embrace.

Later, she knelt in the bathroom, her head bent

under the taps so that the stream of water struck her on the back of the neck. This was how he found her when he came in, carrying their baby.

She took the baby in her arms and held it. Water ran over the faces of the mother and child.

They sat before the television with the baby. The crib had been set up nearby. It rocked gently to and fro. The baby stared out at the mother and the mother stared greedily into the baby's eyes, while the man played music for the words that neither of them could really understand:

> The little boy lost in the lonely fen,
> Led by the wandering light,
> Began to cry; but God, ever nigh,
> Appeared like his father in white.
> He kissed the child & by the hand led
> And to his mother brought,
> Who in sorrow pale, thro' the lonely dale,
> Her little boy weeping sought.

The father played this with many mistakes, and when he was finished, she told him.

"This isn't our child," she said, in a slow deliberate voice. "His eyes are not the same; see, they're blue, plain blue. Those aren't Richard's eyes."

The man groaned and put his face in his hands. "It can't be," he said, shaking his head slowly. "It can't be."

"I'm going to call him Sargon," she said. "That name is in the book too. If we're going to have a new child, he must have a new name."

The man closed his eyes. He couldn't think of such things anymore; he had been through too much. After a while, however, he seemed to recover a little, and they all watched television together, waiting for the fabulous guests.

Captain Flynn

In an old house, part of an estate not far from the famous European town, she met Captain Flynn. Because she had been told to, she had taken her clothes off, and her tiny bare white feet stirred up no dust, even when she moved from the polished wood floor to one or another of the thick oriental carpets that made pleasant islands between the mirrors and the shapely divan.

Standing on the central one of these carpets and looking south, she could see through the double glass doors into the orangerie, where faint, moist blooms stretched and wavered in the spare sunlight. Turning her head to the right, she took in the painting of the serpent and wondered at the way its arched diamond body seemed to have been nailed, or rather jewelled, into the panelled wall. From this same position, out of the corner of her right eye, she was aware of the mirror behind her, aiming back at her some semblance of her own flesh, quite white in this aspect, twisted, and poised there as if held in readiness for something. Looking to the left, finally, she could survey the very long, low, pink sofa, a generous but palpable lotus, on which floated the still sleeping, splendidly naked body of her host, Captain Flynn.

If it had been up to her, she would have continued staring straight ahead, for the orangerie was certainly full of pleasant shapes, and highlights enough for any eye; the longer she looked at it the more clearly she could distinguish one beauty from another. For example, several thickly clustering large purple climbers caused her no end of amazement, so lush they seemed, so soft hanging there and yet sturdy and profuse. And also a number of cactus-like plants with sharp angular needles and little bunches of pink flowers at the tips. And the bamboo trees and the magnolia, and a specimen that must have been one of the bougainvillea—all so intriguing!

It was not only the plants, but the sculptures in the wonderful orangerie that held her attention, at least for that little while. She could make out two of the pieces quite clearly. One was the gaunt naked figure of a man, life-sized, turned upside down and apparently crucified in that position, like St. Peter. It was a bronze sculpture, quite naturalistic, but distorted and angular, held in place by crossed quartz-like pins that supported the figure while at the same time giving the effect of crucifixion. Nearby, the cactus needles shone in a nicely calculated rhythm of continuation, and the whole area glittered as if lit with tiny altar candles.

The other sculpture was a large sphere, possibly six feet in circumference, and so transparent that it brimmed with constantly shifting beams of light. Immured dead centre in this sphere was a larger-than-life reproduction of a frog, yet so vital was its presence that it might have been a mutant giant of the species, eerily staring at her.

Luckily, they had warned her not to be disturbed by any of Captain Flynn's works of art, pointing out that though he was an eccentric he must be tolerated, if only because he was so definitely one of their own. Of course she had memorized the message, and was only waiting for the proper moment to deliver it. Yet to determine that moment might be a difficult problem, given that there were no orders, not even any hints on that point from the group itself, so she bided her time, aimlessly staring out at the sunshine, the greenery, and the flowers.

For a while, she even closed her eyes and dozed a bit, only to wake feeling quite rested and refreshed, not least because of the elegant little breeze that all by itself had pushed the double glass doors open. She felt this breeze along the length of her body, which seemed to have fallen into place where she stood, so that she was not tired, nor had her long beautiful legs gone to sleep when she did, nor did her lovely shoulders slump unduly, given that she herself was still very far from being a statue or a sculpture and might reasonably have complained. She could even stretch her arms with impunity and fuss with strands of her dark hair, though she knew that to move her head suddenly would have been overbold.

She was not certain how she first became aware that Captain Flynn was awake. Perhaps, despite the soft rustle of the wind among the plants, she had picked up his breathing, sharpened to a new pitch as he surfaced. Perhaps out of the corner of her left eye, she had caught some slight movement, some faint stirring of that lithe and splendid black body.

However it was, she was allowed finally to turn

her head, and as she did so caught her breath to see those indolent, reclining, almost helpless limbs of the man—leaning back as he was, almost like the shipwrecked black man in Winslow Homer's *Gulf Stream*—suddenly tense and tighten with awareness, and the head, magnificent, leonine, turn just slightly to acknowledge her presence there.

Or so she thought, and remembered that the message, if it was to be given to Captain Flynn, must be given only at his command.

Then she noticed, or noticed again, for she had indeed seen it on her first surveying glance but had let it pass, that as she turned both head and body slightly Flynnward, the tilting gilt mirror above that lotus couch caught her, or rather just the intimate parts of her, and held them there at eye level for the man—at least from her angle.

And at this moment he stretched himself, sending shivers through and along the couch, yawned, and opened his eyes. She waited in a sudden terror of joy and suspense, but when he stirred again he turned inward and away, so that she saw at once both the back of his head and, beyond that, in the mirror, his intelligent perfectly formed face, precisely *vis-à-vis* her most tender parts.

Before she could think what to do, he was leaning

forward, as if to meet her secret fears and wishes, eagerly caressing the adjacent image of her—so it seemed, although he might have been simply yawning at the wall, at the mirror. From her angle certainly his mouth and tongue and lips were on her, and she could not turn back for anything, could not untwist herself, out of modesty, so great was the long surge of pleasure she felt at the sight.

After that first little shock, it never occurred to her to wonder what in fact he might be doing, or to think about what from his angle he might be feeling. It was sufficient to watch that magnificent body twist to reach her, the lips applied to her with a determination so eager and yet so fixed that it made her forget even how to move, never mind think. Indeed, for all that time she was in no danger of even attempting to speak or of trying to see the orangerie, or of demanding an explanation of anything, because her body was slowly waking up to an intensity in which she clenched to herself all her best powers of being just what she was, until the end.

She was nearly there when, with pleasure striking notes on every pulse and her thighs rubbery fine, she saw in her straight-ahead fixed gaze at the wall that he moved, turned, and was about to get up and might even come toward her! Rolling unsteadily and yet blithely, as she was, across a series of crests toward some unimaginable climax, she felt this as cruel indifference, even as a deliberate insult, as a terrible mockery of the complete and open intimacy she had freely given up to now, despite his failure to reassure her by even so much as a wink. He had lain there, it seemed, taking his pleasure with her in his fashion, and now he was cutting out at the very moment she had dreamed of for so long, in dreams that she had refused to tell either her husband or those important persons who had sent her here, curious as they were about her inner life.

So angry was she, so crudely yanked away from a final pleasure so meaningful, that she turned right around, got up, raised both her arms, and started to scream at the top of her lungs, against all the instructions they had so carefully planted in her for so many weeks before. Strangely, however, though the screams came tearing up from her chest through her throat and she could actually feel the emotion as a sudden gagging pressure that came near to choking her on the spot, no sound actually issued from her lips.

At that moment, too, Captain Flynn completed the act of getting up, and stood quivering in every muscle just in front of the pink swell of the sofa. For the first time he actually looked her directly in the face, while her glance ran angrily up and down the splendid, gleaming length of his body, slicked now with the sweat of heavy exertion. All of a sudden, it seemed, he recognized her, his eyes rolled helplessly, his body, tensed with a sullen fire of sexual arousal, dimmed and flattened before her gaze and, roaring, half in pain and half in anger, he shouted at her:

"*There was no word you could have spoken.... None!*"

With a wild shamanic roll of his eyes, before she could even attempt to speak, he whirled, and with one strong black fist smashed the gilt mirror to pieces, falling, as he did, over and across the sofa's bright pink folds, falling away into the darkness, into the unreadable dark space that suddenly loomed there.

And she, for her part, seeing him fall and knowing indeed that there was no word she could have spoken, let herself go, collapsing even where she stood. Helpless there on the rug, she felt the strength running out of her, her rubbery thighs spread around her own dark centre that she could not even see because in falling she had turned away, not only from him, but from herself.

And as she lay there, she saw the snake unpin itself from its jewelled captivity and slowly slither down the wall. She heard the wrenching away of the pins and knew that the crucified man too was waking and coming to life and in a minute would probably enter through the double doors and find her. And then she heard the unmistakable explosion of glass that was not the door but the sphere in the orangerie. A cold, damp odour, as of the deepest earth, pervaded the room, and she heard the gigantic croaking and irregular padded leaps of the frog, which, before she could move or complain, had settled its large webbed feet on her breasts, fastening itself to her with a clammy grip, while it stared down at her with its shining bulbous eyes.

It stared and stared and she could not scream, but she remembered one or two of the things they said might happen to her, if she failed in her visit to Captain Flynn.

Locusts

Nostalgia is a sly demon, my wife had written at the climax of her letter, *as alluring as it is corruptive. We should enjoy only the present moment and distrust everything else. That's the secret to happiness.*

I read this sentence and crumpled the paper in my hands, feeling my wife's presence in the words—her certainties, her enormous confidence, the power with which she dispensed her somewhat limited insights into everything. Too often for me she was an absent body, the object of my unfulfilled desire; now she was simply a voice, writing to me from her comfortable apartment halfway across the world, advising me on how to live.

"Don't let her intimidate you," Holbrook said,

without looking at me, bending further over the map and scratching his short-clipped greying hair. "Your wife, I mean—though she sounds very intelligent. You said she's a writer, didn't you? Is she beautiful?"

I didn't know what to answer; I supposed she was beautiful enough. Some people thought so.

We had stopped for repairs in a wadi just off the main Ta'iz road, some miles south of the Yemeni highlands. (This took place before the country was ravaged yet again by endless warfare). For hours it had been the same: relentless heat, milky white sunshine, an unending hazy horizon, blistered rocky outcroppings, and irregular shifting patches of sand. The very paradigm of emptiness, the Tao of unmeaning. But this sublime scenery was grounded in the everyday: our drivers were busy changing a flat tire.

Ahmad was singing a little song in his own language, the most primitive dialect of the oldest Arabic. The wheel wrench fell and clanked against the jack. Jama laughed and nudged his friend in the ribs. Some sexual innuendo in the lyrics, perhaps.

The sunlight blazed; the air hardly moved. I tried to ignore the heat and the stink of the gasoline. The brandy in my canteen was pleasantly warm, and I took a sip, without offering Holbrook any. After a while I put the canteen down and simply sat there, running my fingers across the surface of the rough grey bag that contained the UNESCO instructions. These authorized us to visit Yemen and make contact with the anti-locust teams that roamed the southern desert. There was some suspicion that one of those teams was stealing rare artifacts from the ancient Bayhan sites.

Holbrook, like me an archaeologist, was a professor hired by UNESCO from a small elite college in Pennsylvania. I rather liked him, or at least felt sorry for him. His son, a young filmmaker, had been murdered in the North African desert. I was certain, however, that on this trip the professor had been co-opted by American intelligence. They were looking for Al-Qaeda training camps in Yemen, hardly trusting the Yemeni government's assurances that its sporadic crackdowns were effective. A couple of very discreet gentlemen from Washington had approached me first, then backed away when they found out that I was a dual national, and much more Canadian than American. If some obscure CSIS file had put them off, the next logical thing would have been to try Holbrook, a close colleague, and, like me, an authority on South Arabian archaeology. He seemed to me a good choice—innocent enough on the surface, naïve really, but competent, and perhaps even sly and sinister underneath.

Holbrook continued to peer at his map, squinting in the sunlight. His concentration was admirable.

As for me...I had none left. I was obsessed with my own life, bleak now and barren as this desert. I thought of my wife and wondered if she had grown tired of her lover. The slender, agile one, the snake—I could never bear to pronounce his name, even silently and to myself. I had the image of a small, smirking man, cocksure in his possession of her sweet body.

A kind of rage seized me, impotent rage. I spat into the sand.

"Are you all right, Dennison?"

Holbrook regarded me with his firm, blue-eyed gaze. It was incredible what a steady look he had. His eyes were such a fine blue. He was what they call "raw-boned," with a strong jaw and large but shapely hands. He was impeccably dressed, of course, in full desert rig, khaki shirt, and soft hat. Distinguished-looking—I had thought so from the first—and impressive, all the better to fulfill his secret mission.

It was ingenious, really. How better to cover the

activities of a spy than by getting him to pretend he was obsessed with something as remote as the planet Mars?

"In the desert I always think of the landings," Holbrook confided. "How surprised we'll all be when the truth is known."

He glanced at me very quickly; I was certain he was trying out his new role. His handlers had instructed him to pretend that he was researching desert life in order to apply his findings to the question of life on Mars. Back in Aden he had spouted a lot about the subject at various parties.

"The first tests, as everybody knows, were ludicrously primitive," Holbrook assured me. "Look at the Yemeni desert, for example; if somebody landed a bottle of water here would anything grow in it? Now we've discovered some very interesting phenomena on what a few are still pleased to call a 'dead world.' I've read all the papers and looked at hundreds of photographs, and there's every hope of finding life on Mars. We know about the dry riverbeds, the cyclical floods up there—and I'm here to learn more about the earth parallels. Sometimes skepticism goes too far in denial, don't you think?"

I nodded dutifully. I wondered if his palaver was also for the benefit of Ahmad and Jama: it wasn't out of the question that they were spying on us. In this world, everyone seemed to be spying on someone else.

I stuffed my wife's letter in my pocket and wandered away from the jeep.

In two hours we had a rendezvous some distance south with a desert locust team coming up from Lahej. One of them probably had further instructions from the CIA for Holbrook. I wondered what was happening out here in the desert that needed such urgent attention.

Around me was a landscape of moon-rubble and heat-blasted rock. The main vehicle track led northwest toward the now visible foothills of Yemen and southward toward the main seaport, Aden. At this very spot, though, scrub bush sprang up everywhere; the rains that would fall in force later, though intermittently, had already lured clumps of dark-green shrubbery out of the resistant rock. I could see stunted, twisted acacia trees, the red-stemmed abb, thorny plants, and rough grass that looked like a prickly carpet.

Everything was placid and dreamlike. I walked slowly; my boots seemed barely to touch the earth. For the first time I noticed how the black cliffs just ahead of me fractured, making small valleys, dead spaces among the riven rocks. As usual, there was nowhere to go, no thickets or mysterious recesses to explore, just the experience of light flashing on rock, the unrelenting sun.

All of a sudden I had a feeling that something tremendous was about to happen. A cloud of darkness had appeared on the western horizon. It approached us, faster and faster. Ahmad and Jama stood up, pointed at the sky, and danced a few crazy steps. Holbrook was shouting at me. I listened, but it wasn't until I paused, stopped, and looked back at the jeep that I heard it. A buzzing and ticking sounded everywhere, a mad telegraphy, or the endless clicking of the burner mechanism on a thousand gas ranges.

The dark cloud had come alive with small pink blossoms. They fell everywhere, making that peculiar clicking sound as they struck the rock and the hard sand. Some of them crawled away after landing, or hopped about like demented twigs. They seemed to be seeking something, and soon every bush and scrub plant, every cranny, was full of them, moving, struggling, feeding where they might, or spilling down helplessly onto the earth.

We were in the middle of a swarm. Scheduled to meet the locust team, we had met the locusts instead. It was the first time I had ever experienced such a thing, and my early upbringing proved irresistible. I thought at once of the Bible and of the plagues of God. I felt myself at the centre of a visitation.

The insects cascaded down, striking my head and hands, tickling my face, making me close my eyes for a moment and walk blind. I found myself tripping, then laughing hysterically—partially but not wholly at my own inflated thoughts—and as I staggered down the slope toward the jeep I noticed that Holbrook (who had spent more time in the desert than I) seemed to be similarly poised between hilarity and awe. Ahmad and Jama had crawled under the jeep, but the professor was lurching up the rise, heading toward me, waving his arms like a prophet and shouting incomprehensible words—at me, or at the insects, the cliffs, and the sky.

About midway between us lay something I had quite missed on my walk up the slope: a pile of round boulders, nuggets of volcanic rock like huge black eggs. They made a heap that seemed almost like an ancient cairn, although I was certain they could not have been pushed together in this wilderness by any human hands.

Within seconds this rock pile was veined with

shimmering pink as the locusts struck it, swarming over the green shoots in the crannies, falling back into the sand like swollen buds.

Holbrook staggered up to the cairn and I met him there. I was giggling helplessly and so was he. With frantic gestures we brushed away the insects, then spontaneously crouched in the sand.

"Look at them!" Holbrook cried. "Isn't it wonderful!"

"You've never seen this?"

"Never!"

Now everything seemed magnified, and my eyes became a camera in close-up, following the wriggling movements of first one, then another of the insects. As one crawled along near my outstretched hand, I marvelled at its apparent singleness, at the tiny legs, the quivering antennae, the shiny carapace. I wanted to believe that each of these creatures had a will of its own, that it struggled forward according to some individual inner plan. Of course I knew that this was only an illusion, but the idea fascinated me. In this era of control, when everything human seemed to be reduced to mechanism, a belief in insect anarchy was almost comforting.

I reached out and touched the warm stone. I brushed away some locusts and watched them climb toward a crack full of green shoots. Perversely,

I tumbled them down into the sand, pulling out the grass shoots as I did so.

Hunger, the real essence of life, I thought—and here was hunger in its most primal form.

Holbrook stood close beside me. He bent over, and amid the clicking and the low whirring sound of the swarm, he started speaking.

"You know why I'm here, don't you, Dennison? I mean what my real mission is? It was clear to me from the first that I couldn't deceive you. I suppose you despise me for working with those people—it doesn't surprise me."

I shook my head and said nothing.

"I've made a decision to come clean—not to tell you anything much of course, but just to clarify the situation between us. I can see that you couldn't care less about politics: terrorists, anti-terrorists, who's paid to spy on whom, which fanatics are playing what game. Your personal story, your sad little love story—oh, I don't means to belittle it, or to deny you your misery!—but your own story, I know, trumps everything."

I gritted my teeth, and nodded. "I guess you've found me out," I told him.

"Only because we're brothers under the skin," he said. "I don't give a damn for all their politics either.

I might care, just as you might, if real suffering innocence was involved, but we know that isn't the case. It's terrorists on all sides, really, isn't it?"

I reached down and brushed away a few more locusts. "Then why bother? Why compromise yourself? Why get involved in their silly, brutal games?"

Holbrook laughed—a dry, hollow laugh. "Look!" he said. "Look all around you. Look at the locusts. The swarm. The unthinking swarm. They move according to laws that we pretend to understand, to control. But we control nothing. We understand nothing. Our lives are just a flash of vision, a moment of illusory freedom, before the darkness. Politics is just a mirage, an abstraction, an attempt to control life and society, one that always fails."

"You're thinking of your son," I said, sensing the source of his bitterness, his disillusionment.

He didn't answer. Then his expression changed, and he pointed at the rock, swarming with the insects. "Look, Dennison! What have you found?"

I thought that his excitement had passed all bounds, that he had really gone out of his senses. Then I looked at the rock again. I stared at the spot where I had pulled out the grass, and saw something so utterly unexpected that I had to touch it once, twice, three times, to confirm its reality.

A picture had been scratched on the stone, an image gouged deep in the rock itself, quite clearly a pair of human figures.

Had someone left a pictorial message for us in this wilderness? Or was I really as obsessed as Holbrook? Was I just another powerless soul, desperately in search of something meaningful?

Examining the image, however, I saw at once, with the instinct of many years in the field, that this was a genuine petroglyph, and possibly quite ancient. The style was familiar enough, but the subject was unexpected.

The incised figures were not large—only about five or six inches long—but carefully chiselled in the rock by some primitive implement, and clearly visible, although much obliterated by time and weather.

The carving depicted two bodies coupling. This was already unheard of in the south Arabian archaeological context, but the real shock came when I noticed that the figures were not simply a man and a woman, but a voluptuous woman being ridden by a creature only half human, a satyr-like figure with horns, the suggestion of a leering face, and a hugely exaggerated sexual organ.

The figure of the woman depicted in a state of lethargic tension was a precise embodiment of the universal oxymoron of sexual yielding-giving. Perhaps just for this reason there was something utterly convincing in her simple brazen pose.

Holbrook seemed beside himself. He was an archaeologist more truly than he was a spy, and now he was looking at something rare and precious. He had made a discovery—and he gave a little shout of triumph. I slammed my fist in the sand, stood up, and gazed around me. Ahmad and Jama were lounging by the jeep, laughing and pointing at the rocks and the bushes.

I couldn't say a word. I was suddenly in the middle of my own sorrow, my heart was consumed again with jealous rage. I heard my wife's laughter and saw her face, alive with pleasure and renewed mockery.

In an excited voice, from somewhere far away, Holbrook said, "Don't you see? It doesn't fit the local style! Yet it's so familiar…universal, in fact. Once in the Sahara I came across something analogous, an offshoot of the pre-Carthaginian…. The Sahara… that's where my son died, I think you know…."

He paced across the sand, and continued, "My son…. Yes, he was murdered in the desert. Murdered by some local thieves for the sake of his cameras and equipment. Wiped out, obliterated, for what?

For almost nothing! A life worth more than any politics! A terrible thing, but in fact he'd always been obsessed with death. That's why he travelled in dangerous places, and always alone. He was throwing out a challenge—to himself, to fate—God knows why! It was foolish, of course, and very human. Now—as he wished—his body is preserved in a cryogenic tank in a suburb outside of Chicago. A kind of immortality.... But it's all pathetic, it's a swindle. Just disgusting, that place—those zombies and corpses, floating in chemical sewage. Not clean, like the desert. And there's nothing—not a thing—that I've been able to do to change what happened. I'm helpless, swept along by life, incapable even of his gesture.... I don't care about politics, about anything. I just want to forget."

I could find no way to console him. My glance swept from the rough stone, with its faint, mocking scrawl, to the scene around me. The locusts were beginning to gather, to pass on. I watched them as they coalesced slowly into a great amorphous mass. They were fluttering together, taking shape as a dark cloud, and within a few minutes they had left us. I shielded my eyes and followed their flight to the east. Once again they had turned into something collective, and at the same time insubstantial, a faint shadow moving across the empty land.

We stood there, Holbrook and I, not speaking, barely glancing at each other, trapped by our memories, our regrets. All around us the desert had been stripped of its thin green life, and the harsh sun glinted on bare rock and sand.

Massenet and the Disappearing Sopranos

Whose life is ever complete? Events make distant echoes, and the past is continuously replayed, even for the dead. The composer we know as Jules Massenet, famous for his sentimentally appealing operas and his fondness for beautiful sopranos, died in 1912. What follows takes place partially in the past, and partially in a future that meets that past only as fiction, here in the form of this story.

Massenet, once again exactly forty-one years old, has just written *Manon*, that opera of male passion, self-deceit, and innocent female opportunism, and as usual is awaiting at a distance the verdict of the audience of the Opéra Comique. Although he has often gone to the rehearsals of his operas, making sure that this or that detail is quite correct, and sometimes changing the score on the spot to accommodate necessity, he makes it a point, out of superstition, never to attend the actual premieres of his own works.

As he sits comfortably at home in the village of Avon before his private viewing system, preparing to watch his new opera on a specially built screen, Massenet is nonetheless very nervous. The busy, quite plain maid has come and gone, leaving behind half a decanter full of a pleasant Beaujolais.

Ninon, his wife, has carried her knitting away to her own room, and will no doubt make an appearance, for politeness' sake, at the perfect moment, when she is sure all is going well. Massenet decides to turn off the sound on the pre-performance chatter that will rehearse his career, his accomplishments, his failures and trials, almost as if he were a dead man. He is thinking, with some passion, of a peculiarly touching moment during those first days at Vevey, of Sybil standing against the large double doors of the hotel suite, the gold, orange, and pink light of a spectacular sunset pulsating around her and making her look like a flower in the centre of a cyclorama.

Sybil Sanderson he had met one evening just as he was slipping away resignedly from a boring dinner, which he had only decided to attend at the last minute.

A handsome older woman approaches and introduces herself. She is from Sacramento, California, resident in Paris; her husband, who has recently died, was a justice of the American Supreme Court. Would Massenet listen to her daughter, who is studying with Marchesi, and who, claims her mother, is amazingly talented?

Massenet is inclined to give in, noting how well preserved is this older woman, in her deep midnight gown of gathered tulle—a shapely, stately woman who speaks French with only a slight and charming accent. But when he sees the daughter, the composer melts: she is very young, and extraordinarily beautiful, with lovely skin and dark-flowing, gold-toned hair, gestures that strike deep, and transfixing eyes. (It is nothing that now and forever, thumbing through the many biographies written after his death, the composer pauses, stares, and wonders what he really experienced that night. In this he is no different from any of us, who fail to capture the truth in that mirror in which time is constantly dissolving certainty. The composer continues to note with puzzled affection the disappearance of all his sopranos, the transparency of all his many sincere disguises—as we may, thinking of our own.)

Yet when she sings for a moment in that gilt drawing room crammed with eternal projections, Sybil is Queen of the Night. "Lower to upper G," notes Massenet, "three octaves—splendid! And what fine control. Also, she has fire and intelligence. Just look at the eyes! What promise for the stage! I'm convinced."

The next day he decides she is just right for the new role of Manon, or Esclarmonde, or Cendrillon, and starts to work on the score with tremendously renewed intensity. A few months later they are vacationing together in Switzerland.

They stay at the Grand Hôtel de Vevey—Massenet, Sybil, and her mother, who is going blind. The weather is crystalline, the mountains reassuringly theatrical. Massenet writes feverishly and fills up pages of his diaries with large-scrawled script, out of which the letter S rises obsessively, an emphatic treble clef for his song of passion. Meanwhile, there is much salon music, tutoring, many handkerchiefs, trembling hands, sighs, dreams, and, finally, a seduction, achieved with the appropriate complicity of both mother and daughter, the former blindfolded, the latter with her eyes closed. Yet the composer once again confronts that always familiar, ever strange dark gulf in which something nearly known continues to escape him. Soon after, the soprano begins to have doubts about her ability, decides to give up the part altogether, and is reconciled to her duty only at the expense of many scenes. So the vacation continues, and the composing, while Massenet's wife and their daughter spend the summer elsewhere.

Ninon, of course, doesn't really count, though he has been careful, through the years, with his swooning over the ladies, and doesn't carry things far enough to drive her to desperate measures. Some inner genius has enabled him to calculate how much she will put up with to a very precise degree, and he always goes as far as he can for his pleasure, but not far enough to lead to the inconvenience of a major falling out with her. Of course, he has been from the beginning a true Romantic, ever requiring some particular embodiment of the muse to be at hand before he can edge himself into real creativity. Perhaps he was inoculated into this fevered rhythm of existence when he won the *Prix de Rome*, and spent some marvellous time in Italy visiting the salon of none other than the great Liszt himself.

Massenet could never forget one of those nights in that city. It was January, and he and some of his friends, out for a stroll, had stumbled, quite by accident, into what seemed to be a vast ruined basilica, whose lurching arcades and coffered vaults teetered crazily against the murky sky. Stumbling forward, perhaps a little drunk, he saw, just above his unsteady line of sight, the spectre of a huge cross shining dimly from the darkness. He looked up at an infinity of blank sky and, peering around him, realized for the first time that he was completely encircled by colossal walls. His friends had meanwhile disappeared, and the immense and terrifying silence was disturbed only by his footsteps, as he hurried past great fallen lumps of statues and ancient cracked blocks of stone resembling ice in which even the faintest gleam of light had been snuffed out. But whichever way he turned, he seemed to find himself back in the centre of the impossible maze. A clock chimed in the distance, and at that moment the lurid, vulgar clang of Liszt's *Totentanz* rang in the young man's ears. Terrified, he lay down on some half-dilapidated steps, put his hands over his ears, and crouched there in stiff terror until he eventually went to sleep.

Dawn came, chilly but releasing. The sharp winter light pointed his way out of the Colosseum, the magnificent ruin that for one night the composer had shared with the cats of Rome.

That very day he met his future, present. and eternal wife, Constance de Sainte-Marie, who is called Ninon. It was a fine romantic idyll. Massenet gave her piano lessons and pursued her for many months, until at last she yielded to his wishes and married him. The ceremony took place in early October in a little church in Avon, and while the priest lectured the young couple and their guests on the Christian duties of marriage, a flock of sparrows whirled, danced, and darted, chattering so noisily outside the gleaming decorated windows that it was almost impossible to hear what he was saying.

Massenet managed to remain faithful to Ninon for a few years, but then formed his first liaisons with various pretty Paris shop girls, and became insatiable. His manner during all of his lives has been that of the "king-baby," the grown-up child sensualist who allows himself to be mothered by his wife—and all women—in exchange for a cooing placidity of manner that is unfailingly amiable. Leon Daudet compared him to a child—or a lapdog—strutting and pawing his way through the drawing rooms with an insatiable eye for the ladies, always expecting to be petted for every incidental display of chivalry, helplessness, or musical talent. Then, finally, when from time to time he achieved his goal and found himself in the arms of this or that ideal woman of the moment, he was surprised. Having convinced himself that he really cared about her, he found it difficult to understand why, at the climax of sexual pleasure, he seemed to look into a blind, dark gulf, how at the supposedly perfect moment of this liaison or that there was nothing personal, and whatever lady it was would vanish in a storm of bliss that seemed to obliterate her personality altogether, so that those qualities that had drawn him into the intimacy were never farther away than when the intimacy was complete. Snared by the fine silk sheets of those Parisian and Swiss hotels, he enjoyed a succession of female bodies that became springboards carrying him into the cold, fiery regions of intimate space. There he could spin on a wheel of pleasure, always circling around a face that the final climax was destined to obliterate forever.

In this incarnation of his story, one of the many times he has watched the premiere of *Manon*, he begins to be very pleased with himself, astonished that anyone should have such a talent as he, suddenly listening to his music as a delighted stranger might. (But he fails to notice in the distance, outside, around the countryside of Fontainebleau, the first stirrings of thunder, the hints of an approaching storm.)

The curtain goes up. The composer adjusts his set. It is a terrifying and beautiful moment; he hears all those melodies by now so familiar to him that he can hardly bear to listen to them. He winces, but the thing—his own creation—is moving now, unstoppable, a headlong river of sound that he fears may suddenly trickle away under the stony resistance of an audience that in the end will dissolve in laughter and mockery.

But no; for now at least there is respectful silence. The orchestra plays with precision; Danbé, the conductor, seems to have things in hand. Massenet sits back, a little more relaxed, sipping his wine, watching the inn courtyard materialize before him.

What is Collin scowling about? Bretigny has nothing to scowl about at this point! The composer makes the first of many mental notes; tomorrow there will have to be corrections, adjustments. (But he fails to notice that the storm around the house has grown powerful; he fails to notice the staccato lightning, the shudders of thunder.)

Ninon has put down her knitting; she has gone in search of the maid. In a minute they will be making their rounds, checking that all the shutters are closed. In a minute they will come into the room where Massenet still sits oblivious, enthralled by the arrival of the coach carrying Manon.

Sybil steps out of the coach wearing that perfect look of youth and innocence that he has been coaxing from her for months. Soon, as the composer well knows, it will be transformed into an expression of longing for the great lyric life of passion, and those brilliant cosmopolitan scenes. The catalyst will be the unfortunate Des Grieux, who will take advantage of the fact that Guillot's carriage is available to rush Manon off to Paris, where their tragic story can begin to unfold. As he watches the familiar features of his beloved express the fresh nuance of every moment, and sees the intimately known body move lightly in its sheath of plain grey wool, Massenet is once again astonished at the ability of his protégé to assume a role. So powerful is the unity she has established with the character of Manon that she seems now almost to have become another person. If it were not for the voice, that divine, incomparable voice....

But suddenly the unity, the heavenly perfection of the rapport is broken. Ninon and the maid burst into the room with jarring cries about the storm, the thunder. Startled, Massenet begins to struggle to his feet. All at once the lights go out everywhere.

"Damn!" cries the composer, knocking over the decanter and blinking helplessly at the lumpish and unyielding darkness. The power supply has been cut off, and unless it returns he will see no more of his precious Manon that evening.

It does not return. Massenet, frustrated beyond measure, prowls about nervously, maintaining an outward calm and his usual polish of manner, but inwardly raging. Soon, having settled Ninon down and made inquiries about the cause of the disconnection, he comes to the conclusion that he must go at once to Paris. There is little chance power will be restored that night, but the storm has passed, and the house seems to have been spared fire or accident. If he takes a fast transport vehicle he will just make it to the Opéra in time to receive the plaudits of the audience, which he is now inwardly sure must love his new work. But what a provoking situation nonetheless! To miss the greatest performance of his dear friend in a role that he had fashioned with the very tissues of his heart! It was unkind, the unkindest thing fate had so far afflicted him with!

The trip to Paris that night occurred without incident, but with much soul-searching by the composer as he sat in the privacy of his special compartment. Already he had some ideas for a new opera, for several new operas. It would only be a question of choosing the one that would do full justice both to his own talent and to the wonderful voice of his incomparable Sybil. And from time to time on that trip, as the lights flickered around him and the night sky stretched away before his glance like the grand stage setting it could often be, the composer allowed himself to imagine what precise point his *Manon* had reached. Would they now be listening entranced to the dainty orchestral minuet that opens the third act? Would Des Grieux be singing mournfully of the haunting memory of his beloved, "*Ah! fuyez, douce image, à mon âme trop chère*"? Surely that moment would wake up that filthy fat bourgeois in the fifth row, who by this time was drooling and fantasizing over his own shabby embodiment of the composer's beautiful heroine. *Ah, Manon, they must all love you by now; they must love you even as I love you, as I have always loved you,* sighed the distracted composer, shaken more than he could say by the night's strange events, and due to be shaken even further, a fact he actually intuited even then, through many dimensions of time, in the experience of so many varying scenarios of his life.

Once in the Opéra, released from the secret unpredictable life of the streets, Massenet was at home. He knew everyone, and nodded confidently to porters, stage hands, third assistant directors, costume ladies, and extras, convinced by the specific nuances of their startled surprise that the opera was over, that it was a success, but that he had much to hear about in the way of misadventures. Danbé, he feared, had been responsible for a few blunders, or the lighting had failed at some point—some minor catastrophe that would amount to nothing in the triumph of the evening. For a triumph he knew it must be, as he penetrated deeper into the arcane private regions of the Opéra, and everyone who recognized him called out respectful congratulations, or actually stopped to bow and clap their hands in enthusiastic tribute. Before long the composer was virtually surrounded by a host of grateful and excited well-wishers, including a few distinguished patrons of the arts, whom he recognized, and to whom he addressed a brief but far from perfunctory bow of thanks. He did not stop, however, but went on in search of Sybil, in search of Danbé, in search of Talazac, who he was sure had made a superb Des Grieux.

At last, turning down the corridor that led him to the very holy of holies, the dressing room area itself, by this time caught up in an excitement that he felt reflected on him from all sides, the composer walked straight into several principals from the opera, still half in costume, led along by the ebullient Danbé.

"A success, Maestro, a wonderful success," the conductor beamed, hardly able to contain himself, and almost taking the liberty of pounding the dignified composer on the back.

The cast crowded around, offering congratulations, and one of them, incredibly, was dressed in the prison rags of the fifth act, the rags Manon herself wears as she dies in the arms of Des Grieux. A musical phrase shot all at once through the startled composer's brain: *Soon our happiness of old will come again.* The whole pathos of the death scene assaulted him and, combined with the unusual emotions of the night, nearly started a quite uncharacteristic fit of weeping.

But who was this dressed up as Manon? It was not Sybil, not his beloved Sibyl, but Marie Heilbronn, whom he recognized at once, a beautiful Parisian soprano, noted for her fine acting and for her scandalous life offstage.

At once Marie seized the arm of the startled composer and, bursting into tears, confessed, *"It's the story of my life...my own life!"*

"She was exquisite, Maestro, exquisite," Danbé assured the dumfounded Massenet. "The whole audience wept at the end."

Massenet raised his arm weakly, blinking at the strange half-painted faces that surrounded him, unreal faces made harsh by the glare of lights from above.

"But Sybil, Madame Sanderson...." The composer could barely get the words out. "She was...taken sick?"

"Unfortunately she couldn't sing at all tonight," Danbé explained patiently. "An accident at the last minute. She sprained her ankle. You didn't know?"

The composer detected a sudden tension around him, as if something vital were being concealed. But Danbé, seeming to sense Massenet's confusion and suspicion, hastened to reassure him, "Of course, Madame Sanderson would have been superb, Maestro. But think, such a substitute at the last minute! It's a triumph!"

The composer looks into the eyes of Marie Heilbronn. He has seen her many times, but now he feels himself drawn to her as never before. She stands there, soft even in the unsparing glare of light that assaults them. Massenet thinks of how perfect she had been as he watched her from Avon, mistaking her for Sybil.

He must go to Sybil now. But Manon is here.

Massenet bends to kiss the soprano's hand. It is a tribute to the real Manon, whoever she is. But already the composer has ceased to think of his opera, his wonderful opera. Already, under the influence of the evening's events, a new inspiration is awakening. For this beautiful woman who has saved his opera he will write the perfect, the incomparable role. This time, of all times, he feels himself on the track of some great wordless truth, capable of almost any depth of profound communication through the music that is beginning to stir in him.

Massenet turns with a light step, trying to call to mind Marie Heilbronn's address and the name of her most recent lover. Surely this time there would be no darkness, no blackout at the heart of the storm.

Rendezvous

Once upon a time, when I was a mere forty-five years old, I was invited to be a guest of honour at Cosmicon VII, that most obscure gathering of Canadian science fiction fanatics. That was not too long after the days of Hippie Heaven, free love, and perennial pot, a time when universities were Pleasure Domes unfettered by deconstruction, deficits, or PCs of any kind.

The site of the Con was the university where I taught, in the Residence Commons Building, shoved off to one side of our sprawling campus near a deserted, half-excavated construction site. The site was always under some kind of litigation, so it remained shabby and marginal. Male students who lived on the upper floors of the residence wing often stood at open windows and urinated onto the dry, caked, brown mounds below; others played Frisbee on the scrub grass, or in mid-winter indulged in half-drunken snowball fights on the Siberia-like sandlot. One visitor, arriving by taxi, took a look at the place and said it would make a pretty good UFO landing pad.

Actually, the Con had been kicked around town, popping up nastily in hotel after hotel like a radioactive tribble. It had started at the Holiday Inn, but a couple of Imperial Storm Troopers got into a disagreement in an elevator, terrifying an old couple from Saskatchewan who were related to the former Governor General. The manager took the complaint very seriously, for there had been other incidents: a Squid Head had been bounced from the Oyster Bar for jumping out from behind the fish tanks and shouting, "The force is with you!" and generally trying the patience of the well-heeled customers; then, too, there were a lot of strange chanting noises coming from the meeting of the Society for Creative Anachronism on the thirteenth floor: they refused to answer their phones or let anyone enter the suite except the red-liveried doorman, who had to knock three times and call out the names of their cocktails in pig Latin.

The following year the Con moved to the Westin. Things were OK there until a rumour started up that Isaac Asimov was arriving on the penthouse roof in the famous Brunner-Monde hot-air dirigible, first tested in Zanzibar in 1934. There was a mad scramble to get out of the building, maybe because of some latent memory of the Graf Zeppelin, or possibly because the Con gang wanted a better view. Unfortunately a visiting Pekinese was killed in the ensuing riot, and the next year the Con had to move again, this time to the Skyline.

Alas, just about then the good old-fashioned SF crowd was being heavily infiltrated by the fantasy buffs, and there was so much iron-pumping and Tae Kwon Do before breakfast that the building shook, while the number of females in leopard skins and prehistoric bikinis led to a night raid by Women-Kind, a local feminist organization that had trashed at least one newsstand that displayed skin mags at eye level.

So, in its seventh year, obviously because a little breathing space was needed, and in response to the universal hotel blacklisting, the Con moved into my own bailiwick. New organizers had replaced the previous gang, who had fled to the Caribbean with all the liquid funds, and they were determined to get things right. The latest venue included an exciting film series (all the Fritz Lang silents, *Things to Come*, and the uncut version of *Solaris*), a debate between Hal Clement and a local priest on evolutionism versus creationism, and a pioneering critique, one that foreshadowed the grim future of academe: a computer-monitored semiotic analysis of the shifts in the pictorial grammar of *Lost in Space.*

Unfortunately, my life was pretty well in ruins by that time, and I just couldn't get into the spirit of things. Several senior members of my Ph.D. advisory board had died of old age and I still hadn't finished the first chapter of my thesis. Nobody was enrolling in my SF course, and I'd been kicked off the university's parking committee for non-payment of tickets. To top it all, just the previous week my wife had announced she was leaving me and taking the kids. It seems that her shrink (whom I had never met) finally decided that I was hopelessly "ungrounded," on the grounds that three years earlier I had confessed to having a flying dream in which I never came back to earth. Now I was being shot down, exiled to a shabby rented room, on late nights reduced to sneaking home and creeping up the stairs so as not to disturb my landlady, who would be sniffing coke with one of her "gentlemen callers" and making bad jokes about the Real Thing.

Because of my depressed state of mind, I had tried

to beg off participating in most of the Con events, and, in fact, late on the first afternoon I was hiding out in my office and wondering if I could skip the fun entirely. But at that moment I was visited by an amazing apparition.

It was a girl, as we used to call them, shunted along to me by one of the department secretaries, just because it was Friday and nobody else was in sight. She was only in town for a few days, I was told, and I was supposed to advise her about transferring to our university from somewhere else—a bit of a joke, for I knew nothing about transfers, credits, regulations, prerequisites, or anything else that had to do with the formalities of enrolment. Having got the word that she was on her way upstairs, I edged to the door, preparing to beg off, to tell her to come back on Monday, to get rid of her somehow so that I could wallow a little longer in my own miserable reflections before slipping on down to the Con.

My notion changed, though, when I opened the door. There stood a tall, slender young woman with sharp, dark-blue eyes, glossy dark hair, and skin that looked soft even in the harsh office light. It took some time to convince her that I really was a professor, but I was soon telephoning all over the place, trying to figure out how I could get her enrolled in the biology and physics courses she seemed to want.

She sat there at my desk, not exactly smiling, but with a strong energy of attention, telling me about her childhood in the wide open spaces, her weird family, how she wrote far-out poetry for fun and had taken up skydiving so as to be able to compete with her athletic brothers and sisters. I listened in a kind of trance, intensely aware of the strange currents that seemed to be flowing between us in that hot little room, hardly paying attention to the details of her account, forming my own idea of her as an unspoiled prairie child who had arrived just in time to save me from the dreariness of the Con weekend.

Her name was Circe, she told me. She pronounced it in what she claimed was the Greek manner, as "Kirky." (*Kirky*? *Kirk*?) For a frightening moment I thought she was going to tell me she was a Shatner-*Star Trek* fan, but no—she had two sisters with equally poetic monikers, namely Cybele and Cassandra. Choosing "C-words" as girl-nomenclature was apparently a family tradition.

I nodded and sat nearly speechless as she gazed round dreamily at my collection of space posters, reaching out to trace with her delicate fingers the lines of an ice-rimmed crater on Titan.

"You like science fiction?" She murmured the question, suddenly bringing her head down and close, as if she were peering into the mechanisms in my skull. I later realized this was characteristic of her whole clan.

"Well, I've been teaching it for a few years," I responded warily, never sure how people would react to the subject, and wanting very badly a favourable reaction from her.

"I don't know much about it—at least not theoretically," she said bluntly. Then, smiling, "Maybe I should take your course?"

I gulped and nodded enthusiastically, fighting off an impulse to invite her to go with me to the Con. My mind worked anxiously; I realized I would almost certainly be hopelessly depressed by all the exciting events of the evening and I didn't want her to think I was some dreary academic, stumbling and blundering through a mid-life crisis that would last for the rest of my life. I wanted her to think of me as she obviously did that very moment: as a sexy mentor, a live wire, a discovery, a connection of promise. I was hoping she just might latch onto my overcrowded and chaotic little office as the brave new world of her next life-adventure. I wanted us to fly, not to sink down drearily into a morass of Conan comics, computer games, and tasteless imitations of Frank Fascisti paintings.

"Look," I said at that point, struggling to muster my most casual and man-of-the-world air, "I gather that you'll be in town for a few days. It's just possible something may come up in connection with all these courses you want to take. Saturday isn't a total loss around here. Why don't you just leave me your phone number, and I'll give you a ring tomorrow or the next day? Maybe we can have lunch and talk about science fiction and your future as an avant-garde poet who specializes in skydiving."

"I'd like that," she said at once in her no-nonsense way, and proceeded to write down a number on my scratch pad. I watched her tapering fingers move, and enjoyed the lovely curve of her neck; then she looked up, fixing me suddenly with her glittering blue eyes and handing me the paper.

"You may have a bit of trouble getting through; we have an elaborate switchboard system—but don't be put off. I'll be expecting to hear from you."

She rose, and slid away to the window, where she stood outlined against the blazing orange light of the sunset. She gazed—not down on the panorama of river and park (my office was on the nineteenth floor of the Arts Tower), but up at the pink-bellied clouds, where a silent, silver-winged plane climbed and vanished.

"I guess I should split," she said, quickly turning, smiling sideways at me as she drifted past, and playfully flicking the edge of my lapel as she slipped out the door.

I watched her move down the narrow hall. The force that had held us both in a shiver of delicious tension dissipated. Left alone with my posters, I strutted around the room, I danced. "A little bit of Kinski," I murmured, crazily articulate, "a dash of Brooke Shields. Maybe a soupçon of Daryl Hannah. And yet so pure, so unspoiled. An angel in J. Crew duds! I want more of this!"

It took me only about three minutes to plunge from the ecstatic to the abysmal, however: I knew I had obligations at the Con. I pulled myself together, gathered up a few rough notes and programs, and made my way into the labyrinth.

This is no figure of speech. Our university, whatever its failings, can boast of a truly marvellous system of tunnels, a spreading network of pathways running deep underground, one that connects all the buildings of our extensive campus. Into this maze I now plunged, moving quickly down the bleak sloping walkway, hardly taking in the rough walls, smeared as they are with the graffiti of successive waves of sex-obsessed undergraduates.

The tunnels were almost empty and I hurried along from junction to junction, ignoring the half-obliterated phalluses, the crossed-out oversized bosoms, the bright glaring slogans of the liberated and the reactionary alike. All too soon I reached the Residence Commons and, climbing a few well-worn steps, came into the cavernous hall where the Con itself was visibly stirring to life.

Those familiar with such matters will understand the scene that unfolded before me at that moment. This was no ballroom of some legendary hotel in Paris or Istanbul, but our own homegrown Con, exiled to the margin of an indifferent, half-deserted campus. The guest writers were not Asimov or Ellison or Le Guin, but those somewhat lesser lights, R.J. Barshott, author of a five-thousand page trilogy on the Venus swordfish people, and Guila Dell, progenitor of various sagas in which hemaphroditic dragons gifted with ESP battled the dreaded Black Wizards of Bor.

Neither of these luminaries was visible, of course; in fact, the hall was virtually deserted. A few pimpled teenagers wandered among the comic book racks, some audiovisual equipment was being hauled across the floor, a couple of gofers were arguing with an immense, practically naked man who seemed to be costumed as a Sumo wrestler. As I wandered away from the door one of the gofers ran over and asked me who I was, and though seemingly disappointed that she wasn't registering R.J. himself, handed me a program, a gold guest-of-honour badge, and flashed me a welcoming smile.

I pinned on my badge and fled at once from the hall to the nearby undergraduate pub, which, thank God, was open, tenanted only by a few down-at-heels half-drunken gamesmen arguing about who would play Rommel in the next round of *Panzer Attack Africa*, the latest reconstruction of the good old days of the WWII desert campaign. The TV blared away over the bar—a baseball game in progress—and I got the lady to set me up with several quick ones. Guests straggled in. I continued to drink and things took on a more promising air. My mind was full of Circe-sayings and gestures. As I got more sloshed I could almost feel the girl's breath on my cheeks. I knew that my friend Don, the chief organizer, had set me up with a room in the Residence Commons (one of perks of being a guest of honour), so I kept on drinking and began to fantasize retiring to my appointed cell with my new-found long-limbed beauty.

I don't remember much of what happened next. Somehow I got out of the pub, got hold of a key, and after several attempts to catch a non-existent elevator in the power supply room, found my sleeping pad tucked away in the dark recesses of the upper floors. I sprawled gratefully on the bed, my mind swimming with swordfish maidens who resembled Jacuzzi girls, and hermaphroditic dragons who turned in a wink into Martian princesses.

Then, as they say, everything went black.

I tossed for what seemed hours on a comfortless bed, dim shrieks of laughter and the sound of flushing toilets reverberating in the spaces inside my skull. At last I surfaced, pain hammering my head, my stomach not to be thought of. When I found the courage to get up, I tore my clothes off, crawled into the shower, and lay there gratefully under the pelting stream. Much later, I dragged myself out, consumed several aspirins, collapsed on the bed, and fell asleep.

That's how it happened that I arrived at the Con when it was in full swing, horribly depressed but with an appearance at least of being fashionably roué rather than blatantly dissipated.

Not that it helped much, on the inside at least. I wandered queasily from scene to scene, appalled at the press of bodies, at the sight of numberless devotees, hopelessly hyped up and noisily enjoying themselves in every direction. With a twinge of horror I realized that the old panic was taking hold of me: it was exactly the same feeling as had overcome me at every Con I had ever attended. I was like Gulliver returned from the Houyhnhms, gazing at humankind and finding it suddenly grotesque, or like Wells's Prendick, having escaped from Dr. Moreau's gruesome island, walking the streets of London and seeing the beast peering out from apparently normal faces. For, sharply as I gazed about me, I could not find a single ordinary-looking person in all the eager throng that swarmed through the exhibits and showrooms.

Everyone was either too fat or too thin, too tall or too short, disfigured by pimples, cross-eyed, or with some peculiar twitch of arm or leg that caused one mentally to pull up short, or to covertly stare. It was not a question of the "handicapped" in the usual sense—the "handicapped" are often integrated and touching. This was more like a get-together of oddly-shaped people who had somehow, accidentally, but with an eerie precision, jumbled up their clothing and accoutrements until the result bordered on the shocking.

Everyone sported some strange item of dress that added a note of disharmony to what in a few cases might have been an otherwise normal appearance. I saw checkered scarves with dark suits, long red boots accompanying khaki shorts, eye-patches with jeans; reflecting sunglasses; monocles and top hats; orange hair dyes and nose-rings—each disconcerting in its inappropriateness to the ensemble. The fact was that not a single person in the throng looked anything but repulsive—and my instinct was wholly to avoid all of them rather than to make the slightest effort to strike up an acquaintance. It was the same old story: half an hour of these sights and I longed for a vision of something monstrously ordinary: a prosperous banker in a three-piece, or a suburban housewife, ravishingly normal in her polyester pants suit.

In the midst of all this Don Marshall came up, asked me if I was enjoying myself, and whether I could sit on a special effects panel the next morning.

I winced. Don patted me on the shoulder and bustled away (organizers never have more than two minutes to give you at these things). I had winced with reason, though. Over the years I had had my fill of smart-assed special effects persons, who "just happened to have been standing in the room when

Dino De Laurentis was calling Frank Herbert." To these people scripts were cannon fodder, writers were quaint survivals from the age of Dr. Johnson, and film critics were ignorant so-and-so's, obsessed with such trivia as storyline, psychological depth, and visual coherence. Now I had been roped into actually sitting down with these name-dropping masters of the latex mould and exchanging what, among them, passed for ideas—an astounding and thoroughly nauseating thought.

A crowd welled up behind me, pushing me willy-nilly from the corridor. I passed the Dungeons and Dragons room, dodging a few fourteen-year-old glassy-eyed wizards. I looked in on the first film room, where Lang's *Metropolis* was mechanically plodding along. Then the second, where the crew in *Dark Star* were in hot pursuit of the beach-ball alien. The third room—more beach balls, but this time *they* were doing the pursuing and Patrick McGoohan seemed destined to remain a prisoner for life.

I cut out to the main hall; the crowd parted, and there was R.J. Barshott himself, dressed in a baggy pink check suit, sporting a yellow tie and a leather hat with peacock feathers that looked vaguely Austrian. I could hear his loud, carefully enunciated phrases even above the roar of the fans; he was addressing a small group of autograph seekers in his usual pontifical manner. I didn't envy Don Marshall's job of dealing with the great man's post-conference ire: there was sure to be a twenty-five page letter detailing all the things at the Cosmi-con that had proved unpleasing to the creator of the Venusian swordfish people.

I moved quickly in the direction of the Art Exhibition, avoiding another crowd, one that had gathered around a book table presided over by Guila Dell. I didn't have to look: I could imagine how, in the midst of the eager throng, the bright-eyed little novelist would be scratching out autographs, pawing at her own puffed out, gaudily encased volumes like a cat shifting her litter.

A moment later I was paying dearly for this unworthy reflection. I stood in the centre of the gallery space, surrounded, absolutely engulfed, by panel after panel of electric, luridly glowing representations of both the utterly primitive and the monstrously technological. There was, in all these works, such a wild fervour of activity, such a chaos of motion and colour pressing against the boundaries of the frames, that it seemed as if each would momentarily explode and cover the bare white-tiled floor with a Lovecraftian omelette of viscous and pullulating matter.

What pictures! Crude and impossible spaceships, cities, and robots; muscle-bound warriors, both male and female, half-choked by the tentacles of many-eyed reptilian bubbles; Windigo- and sasquatch-like creatures that might have been scraped off the sides of old Chevy vans; and daubs that defied any description, incoherent messes of colour that looked as if they had been ladled onto the canvas out of some half-cooked primal soup of the imagination.

Fighting back a sudden overwhelming wave of nausea, I started to retreat. Imagine my horror when I turned and found my way blocked by a grinning, bespectacled dwarf wearing yellow jodhpurs, a brightly flowered sports shirt, and a black and red beanie surmounted by a tiny propeller. His shirt, flowing jauntily outside his belt, was covered with buttons flashing slogans: HALLEY-TOSIS, MAPLECON STAR, UNCLE DARTH, HAWKING IS STRINGING US ALONG, and such like. There was no doubt about it: I had run into the Star Stoat.

Actually he called himself something else, but that didn't matter. There was only one way to regard the sudden arrival of this garrulous, insufferable "trufan": it was a disaster. After all, hadn't he nearly started a riot in Philadelphia by reading passages from *Dhalgren* over a PA system atop the convention hotel at three in the morning? Hadn't he interviewed several prominent science fiction writers separately, asking each of them the same questions, and then printing the answers of one under the name of another? Hadn't he called several socially active Nebula and Hugo award winners and, using his best imitation Parisian accent, invited them to address the next meeting of the World Gourmet Wine and Food Society in Addis Ababa? I remembered having heard a rumour that a contract had been put out on the Star Stoat; what surprised me was that the rumour appeared false.

"Well, well, it's the professor," said the Stoat, rubbing his white hands and approaching me the way an expert carver approaches a Sunday chicken.

"In fact, I have to run," I mumbled rather unconvincingly. But nothing could put off the Stoat.

"Before you go you've got to hear the latest," he cackled, and gave a little spin to the propeller on his beanie. Several of his cronies, a strangely assorted bunch of Munchkins, had slipped in behind him, hanging on his every word and blocking the exit, so that it was impossible for me to get away.

"You know where Christa McAuliffe, the teacher, went when the Challenger broke up?" the Star Stoat asked me, beaming. I shrank back.

"ALL OVER FLORIDA!" he shrieked, throwing his arms out in a sudden disintegrative gesture. Behind him, his cronies dissolved in hysterical laughter.

The paintings all around me wobbled and swayed as if they were about to burst apart. I closed my eyes tightly, thrust my fists forward, bumped past the dismal dwarves and out of the room.

Down a long low ramp I staggered, trying not to look at the eager, glassy-eyed faces that rose above the comic book racks and the tables; I knew I had to get out of there, to find my way to the bar, to drink myself into oblivion; or else to get on the phone and call—

"Contact!"

I had bumped smack into Don Marshall, who stood there beaming at me and holding up two fingers as if he had just made a tough corner shot in pool.

"Hey, I was just looking for you, old buddy," he told me. "Can you tear yourself away from this place for an hour or so? I have to run across town to see my girl, Monica. She's at a party in Rockcliffe and I promised I'd drop in when things got under way here.... What's the matter with you, anyway? You look a bit weird. Are you sure you're feeling okay?"

"I'm feeling better by the minute," I said, already looking around for the nearest exit. "Are you leaving right now?"

I cast a hasty glance back up the ramp, half-afraid that the Star Stoat and his gang would come waddling and squirming along after me.

"Let's go, then!" Don, in his no-nonsense way, was already leading me toward a side door.

We drove across the city into the expensive residential district where Ottawa's *crème de la crème* hung out and where Don's girl was partying. I sank back gratefully in the seat; even Don's driving, which had a touch of barely repressed lunacy in it, couldn't spoil my relief. While he explained to me all about his relationship with Monica and how he had to placate her more and more because they never seemed to want to get stoned at the same time, I was trying to figure out how I could avoid returning to the Con with him. Even the prospect of hobnobbing with the tedious rich didn't distress me. At least they wouldn't be wearing black and white beanies with propellers.

Journey's end was a long gravel driveway fringed with shrubbery that gave access to a respectable Tudor-style mansion unpretentiously placed near the east entrance gates of Rideau Hall. Although from where we parked you couldn't actually see the Governor General's noble pile, you could almost feel its reassuringly benign presence, beaming out the light of authority and tradition through the murky late autumn night of the capital.

Inside, there were candles and flowers, and maids dressed in black skirts and little white aprons. There was a ballroom for dancing, a large dining room that easily accommodated several huge tables of food and drink; there were white walls hung up with huge canvases (mostly eighteenth-century landscapes), a massive carved banister leading upward, and an intriguing conservatory with glass panels and doors overlooking a garden.

Don cast me a sideways glance and a wink. "Pretty nice place, huh?"

I almost asked him what on earth Monica was doing here; then I remembered: it was a government thing, and she worked for some minister.

The hostess appeared, an attractive and benevolent forty-something, and led me toward the bar while Don excused himself and went in search of Monica.

I stopped along the way and piled up shrimp, ham, and asparagus on a plate, then drank off a few glasses of champagne and began to circulate among the guests.

Everywhere I looked I saw familiar faces, not for the most part people I knew personally, but faces familiar from the papers, or television—the usual quotient of MPs, ADMs, and local politicians. Then there was the arts crowd, the business crowd, and a few media people, mostly of them already sloshed out of their minds. Yet everyone was dressed just beautifully, the women in formal evening wear, the men in elegant evening jackets.

There was Gerald Montrachet, who had changed ministries so often in the last few months that I couldn't remember where he had recently landed; Hugh Mumsey, a ferocious opposition member from the west; Dr. Greenslaw, who had something to do with some newfangled thing called "the wired city"; Charlotte Besserer, the mayor; Peter Blaupunkt, who ran a chain of department stores; Marie Le Clezio, artistic director of the Nijinsky Ballet; and even Raoul Mitgong, a performing magician who seemed to pop up, like Harlequin, when you were least expecting him.

From a distance I saw Don and Monica engaged in that passionate half-suppressed conversation that lovers are often forced into in public. I waved and Monica grinned weakly, so I didn't attempt to join them, but sat back with my champagne and edibles.

What luck! What a relief! A warm glow enveloped me, and I congratulated myself, content to rest quietly in the elegant setting. Everything was suddenly so reassuring that not even the thought of the Star Stoat's beanies or the gallery's revolting images of the primitive and the future could shake me. Even the notion that tomorrow I would have to pay for it all by returning to the Con to dialogue with the latest hotshots from the world of special effects was less than devastating.

I reached for another glass of champagne. Then a woman came up, fluttering across the crowded room like an elegant white bird. It was the hostess, and I noticed—perhaps it was the drink—that she looked younger and even more attractive and benevolent than she had only a few minutes before.

She sat down, took me by the hand, and asked how I was enjoying myself. I mumbled a few grateful words and she beamed.

Her name was Virgilia, she said, and she was glad to hear I was interested in SF. I watched her pick a canapé off a tray; I was intrigued by something in her grey-eyed glance, by the little mole above the cleft of her breasts, by her delicate fingers and the careless way she brushed loose strands of dark hair from her forehead.

"I have to go and see to my guests, but if you'll wait right here we can talk some more," she said, then patted my shoulder affectionately and tripped away.

I had another couple of champagnes and by the time she returned I was feeling great.

She took my hand and led me around, introducing me to a senator here, a diplomat there. The weight of the party seemed to have shifted; there was a flow of elegant dresses and fancy suits upstairs. Some people were leaving, but not many. There was no sign of Don and Monica.

Somehow Virgilia steered me into a little hall alcove presided over by a rather insipidly domineering marble Apollo. We hadn't said much as yet, but the understanding between us was growing by leaps and bounds. I was holding her hand; she kept squeezing my hand and whispering acid comments about the guests in my ear.

I had yet another champagne. "Like to wander upstairs?" she asked. It seemed a nice kind of provocation.

I moved, a trifle unsteadily, beside her. An immense chandelier glittered above us, like a crystal star. On the stairs she clung to me lightly; the smell of her skin was heady. I reached out for the banister.

In the spacious upstairs hallway, guests were milling about and exchanging confidences (no doubt mostly political) in hushed little conversations. Virgilia asked me to wait while she went to the powder room, which seemed to lie beyond a vast second-floor drawing room at the front of the house. I wandered aimlessly along the hallway: it ran back between the archways and the shut doors, only to disappear in a series of shadowy alcoves at the rear of the place.

I waited; the time dragged; I grew impatient. Had my accommodating hostess abandoned me for another guest?

Meanwhile I noticed that a few of the glittering throng were entering various rooms along the hallway; the crowd seemed to be thinning out. I couldn't help but wonder what was going on behind those closed doors—some gambling for high stakes, perhaps. Or, I thought hopefully, maybe an orgy.

I found myself grinning and smirking at my own image in a huge gold-framed mirror beside a bust of Voltaire. Was I a craven, to be left to cool my heels forever in the antechambers of pleasure? I placed my empty champagne glass delicately on top of the French savant's wig, winked at him knowingly, and boldly swung open the door of the nearest drawing room.

Light glared and for a moment I stood there blinking; then the scene in the room stopped its flutter and froze into a kind of stiff pantomime as I shuddered and stepped back.

What I saw made my head reel. Two grinning hunks, armed with sword and spear, stood arguing over a swooning half-naked girl who lay sprawled on a fat white fur rug. In one corner, jabbering, waving their arms and looking silly and threatening, was a small group of party guests, men and women in evening clothes that were smeared all over with mud. Dripping and gleaming as if they had climbed out of a swamp, they appeared to be placing bets on something, perhaps on the gladiators. Beside this Golem-like crowd crouched another woman, magnificently developed, also nearly naked, her white flesh alive in the light. In one hand she held a big water pistol that looked like a kid's ray gun, while with the other she reached down and scooped mud from a big pail, splattering the guests with handful after handful.

I gasped and tottered backward: what had I stumbled in on? But no one in the room paid any attention to me. Somehow, gropingly, I found the door handle, exited quickly, pulled the door shut, and glanced around the hall. My empty champagne glass slid slowly off the bust of Voltaire; it bounced once on the carpet and lay still, like an iridescent bubble. There was a sound of laughter in the room behind me. I felt as though I might be sick.

This couldn't be happening—a Frank Fascisti painting come to life? I was drunk and I knew it. I had imagined the whole thing.

I saw a bald little man, a local politician, staggering slightly as he leaned close to a tall blonde near one of the brass-handled laundry chutes. I needed to talk to someone, so I took a few hesitant steps toward them, but they were involved in their own thing and paid no attention. There was no sign of Virgilia, and the hall was emptying out fast. It was like a bad dream, a nightmare. Did I have my choice of nightmares or was there some way out of this place?

I tiptoed across the thick carpeting and stopped beside another door. Did I have the guts to open it? I pressed my ear gently against one of the polished wood panels.

From inside came a muffled whirring, the soft nasal whine of big engines. Then a few giggles and screams and the low clang of bells, as if unknown machinery were grinding busily away. I turned aside, shuddering, pressed the palms of my hands on my eyes and kept them there.

When I looked up, I saw the blonde disentangle suddenly from a kiss with the politician. She bent down, pulled the latch, and swung open the laundry chute. Only it wasn't an ordinary chute after all, but a small door, a dark gaping space in the wall.

With a brisk shove, she sent the man flying into the chute, slammed the door, and stood back with a satisfied smile.

The walls bulged and glittered; I was horrified, frightened, and yet weirdly intrigued.

At that moment Virgilia emerged from the front room, looking fresh as a butterfly in her flowing white summer gown. She swept toward me wearing a smile as secret and enigmatic as the blonde's.

A terrifying thought brought my dulled brain to focus: I, not she, was the butterfly, struggling and fluttering in a desperate effort to escape the fate of the politician.

I tried hard to move but felt paralyzed. *Have they drugged me?* I wondered. Virgilia came closer, softly calling my name.

A miracle! I found I could move, and made a wild lunge for freedom. I charged past Voltaire, then a marble nymph, then a whole row of staid landscapes. Down the long hall I tottered, step by step, and found a side corridor that seemed to lead toward the rear of the mansion.

Just in front of me a woman stepped out of a room. She was dressed all in black, and as I rushed headlong she reached out. Bumping past her I caught a glimpse of her frozen, fixed smile, long dark hair, white skin, and cold eyes. She looked like some witch out of Walt Disney—I was suddenly in the heart of a child's nightmare.

I think I screamed then—and at that moment came upon a stairway.

Down I tumbled, hanging on to the banister, slipping and sliding as I descended. On the first-floor landing a little group of guests stood chatting and sipping champagne. At first glance they seemed quite normal, but their glazed looks and whispered conversation as they looked at me gave them away. I turned toward the front of the house. I had to find a way out of this crazy place!

But I didn't dare risk it. There were lots of odd people milling around between me and the front hall, and too many rooms. I might get lost, or be waylaid before I made it to the front door. No, I would fool them all. I would find another way out.

I noticed a small door near the staircase and ducked in. There were more stairs—they must lead down to the basement level. I started to descend, a little more slowly now, but with my heart beating fast. I came down to another door, one that bore a neat sign in bright red letters: NO ADMITTANCE, ENTREE INTERDIT.

I hesitated, then pushed through the door and found myself in a wide, open basement that looked at first a bit like a beer or wine brewery. I was suddenly sober, taking in the curious brightness of the place, the white, sterilized walls, the bulbous metal tanks, and the pipes running everywhere across the ceiling. This was no hideaway bar; it looked more like part of a lab.

I was shaken—it seemed as if I had run into a trap or a dead end. I heard voices on the stairs, one of them Virgilia's, cooing out my name as if she were calling a pet animal.

The basement stretched before me and I ran: I saw machinery everywhere, tuned up to a soft hum.

Voices called behind me, but I ignored them. I walked between two vast, humming vats of something and stood beside a gleaming metal track—it was a kind of conveyor belt system, laid out in a circle, with a branch running back into the far recesses of the place. On one wall rose a giant screen on which green lights softly flickered. And everywhere, poised above the track, there were stiffly projecting metal arms, like miniature work-cranes.

The voices sounded closer, and I could hear Virgilia and others once again calling out my name.

For a moment I held my breath.

Then a click and a long whooshing sound, a sharp scream of terror, and the whole place exploded into life.

The conveyor belts rattled, metal arms shifted, amid groans a small cart rose up from the shadows. Lights flashed, the big screen glowed and sparkled with numbers.

A man in evening dress came plummeting down a long chute from the ceiling, bounced into a cushioning net, and lay there wriggling and screaming. Clamps held him fast and the conveyor belt sprang to life again: he was shunted along, right into the heart of the machinery.

I watched in horror as the metal arms went to work, tearing off his fine clothes, stripping him down until he became a pink quivering blob, then fitting him neatly with new things: an electric green sports shirt, pink shorts, and rhinestone-rimmed sunglasses, the latter ingeniously placed on his upturned, ghastly face.

He was swept round the room at a brisk speed,

then pushed suddenly along the branch track, beneath a black metal box that hung suspended from the ceiling. As he passed under it there was a flash; he screamed, and I ran to him, oblivious for the moment of my own danger.

I stumbled along the track beside him. Despite the rhinestones, I recognized one of the politicians I had seen earlier at the party, but he was changed beyond belief. All suavity had been wiped from his features, and all protest: he grinned up at me with a sharp knowing look, a look of positively idiotic complicity.

I stood back helplessly as the belt swept him on. I saw the cart roll forward to meet him. And at the last minute a steel arm came swinging down and deposited on his stomach (where he could just about reach it with his imprisoned right hand) a black and white beanie surmounted by a tiny propeller.

Then he was gone, whisked away into the dark mouth of the tunnel, launched somewhere into the labyrinthine underworld of the city.

The machinery shuddered and groaned and grew almost silent; still, above its low humming I heard once again the voices of my pursuers, the clanging of some metal object on the metal facing of a door in the near wall.

I stood in shock, but my mind worked: *This is how they recruit them...replacements...being sent to the Con!*

Above me, once again, a chute slid open. I heard a scream and the whoosh of a body. The machinery was starting up again.

Then, not looking backward, I ran. Through the cavernous cellar, through a wild storm of lights and the groaning of engines, I kept running.

Dimly, I remember how in my panic I came upon a little window tucked under one of the old beams of the house. Affixed to it was a metal cover I was able to wrench off from inside. I smashed the window and within minutes I found myself entangled in shrubbery; from there I clawed and lunged my way to freedom, out onto the broad empty lawn, then down the placid streets of Rockcliffe, frantically running, casting fearful glances backward, as if at any moment a long metal hook would reach down and snatch me from safety.

Despite my shock and confusion I knew exactly what I must do. It was no good trying to find Don and Monica—God knows, they were probably already on their way back to the Con, fastened prone on the shuttle, their hands clutching beanies, idiotic grins on their faces.

Or even worse, they might be part of the group that was running this underground railway, this infernal machine that made such a fearful bridge between high and low.

No, my only hope was to contact my blue-eyed princess. With her I could escape from this madness, fly away once and for all from the lunatics and the terror.

To embrace that slender beauty, to lie naked beside her in a plush hotel room—that was just what the doctor ordered.

A few more steps and I found myself emerging from the quieter streets, leaving behind the sedate mansions of Rockcliffe with their long driveways and concealing shrubbery. I came upon a grocery store, a couple of antique shops, shut up tight, and then, at last, a corner pay phone beside a cinema.

I dug out a quarter; my hands trembled as I dialed the number. Suppose she should be out? Suppose she had forgotten who I was?

There followed a series of rings, strange switching sounds, then a pause. I was in despair, but remembered that she had told me I might have some difficulty getting through.

I kept trying, and finally a male voice came on, one with a slight foreign accent. I asked for Circe.

I thought I heard him laugh, but before I could say anything he instructed me to wait. I stood watching helplessly as a police car appeared at one corner and began to cruise down the street; I huddled close to the instrument. The police car slowed down and stopped nearby, and the officers seemed to be observing me from the safety of their vehicle. After a minute or so—it seemed much longer—they drove on.

Finally, I heard Circe's clear voice on the line. I swallowed hard. There was no way to tell her the truth. How could I? But I explained that the SF Con was a bust and that I'd love to meet her, that very night if possible. I tried to sound calm, but she caught on.

"You're in trouble," she said in her quiet way. "Why don't I come and pick you up?"

I was speechless. It was like waking up from a nightmare. Trying to keep my voice steady, I explained where she could find me.

The next few minutes seemed to stretch into hours. But at last I got hold of myself, and having run through all the reasons why she would never come, I caught sight of a sleek black two-seater, cornering sharply, heading straight for the front of the cinema, where I stood pretending to be reading the posters for *Buckeroo Banzai*.

That was odd—I'd been expecting her to show up in a taxi. Despite all my uncertainty, I couldn't help thinking, *So she's rich as well as beautiful.* Well, maybe that made things even better! I greeted her, gaping through the window at her elegant profile, at her body, lithe and slim behind the wheel of that sinewy black curb-blaster.

"Don't try to explain anything now," she said in her flat, gentle voice, leaning over to brush me with a delicate kiss as I settled back blissfully in the cushions. I closed my eyes; the seatbelt was a saving harness and I was just a tired child.

"We'll go to my place," she said, and flipped on some music. I took a deep breath and counted my blessings.

The music flowed around me. I recognized the score, music from *Blade Runner*. Vangelis, I thought, just when I needed you. I dozed, sensing the girl's body, so close and reassuring, then stole a glance at her perfect face, illuminated by the blue, eerie dashboard lights.

I began to surface then, to recover my cool. I was feeling eager, and certainly curious about my lovely companion, who was capturing more and more of my attention, locking up my soul, and drawing me to her with more and more intensity, without any effort, as it seemed, on her part.

"This is some car," I said. "What is it, a Maserati? And where are you staying anyway?"

She didn't answer. I sighed and gazed around. We were approaching the University, turning down from the main thoroughfare onto the long narrow road that ran past the construction site. And there, plain to see, was the horrible Residence Commons, the building that held the Con, the damnable Con that had plagued me and driven me to that even more frightful mansion up in Rockcliffe.

The sight of the place, the sense of what must be going on in there, disturbed me. Hadn't she promised to take me to her pad? What were we doing here?

"*Hey, where are we going?*" I burst out. The old panic rushed up and I turned to her.

But she ignored me, pulling back on the wheel. The car seemed to gather new power. There was a roar, great metal fins appeared on either side of the hood. Moments later we were rising, taking off from the road, from the earth.

I gasped and started to say something to my princess, to the beautiful Circe, but one look at the glittering power in her eyes shut me up.

Below us, the streets winked with light, tall buildings stood out in the darkness.

Up above, dipping slightly from a high bank of cloud, a great silver disc, the brightly lit mother ship, gently hovered. For a moment or two it hung motionless, but then, quite majestically, it descended, slowly approaching our vehicle for the rendezvous.

The Kosi

Martin Bogner, a skinny, grey-haired scholar, with a broad, flat face, a long nose, and bulging eyes, sits in his shabby armchair reading Malinowski. The essay is familiar: "Spirits of the Dead in the Trobriand Islands," and when he finds the passage he is looking for he scribbles down a quotation in his notebook:

For some time after his death, the kosi, or ghost of the dead man, may be met on a road near the village. People are distinctly afraid of meeting the kosi and are always on the lookout for—

A loud knock at the door startles him. Martin groans and shouts "Come in!" He has a feeling it is Cap, but it can't be: Cap the landlord, Cap the boozer, Cap the slob—but Martin's only friend in the world.

Martin throws down his pen and springs across the room, bumping into his wire shopping cart. (He is a familiar figure on Preston Street, in his second-hand clothes that never quite fit, pushing his cart along, shouting at the kids who insist on smoking in the bus shelters.) Now his cart topples over, and his files—which he carries with him everywhere, since the house is such a firetrap—spill out all over the floor. He swears loudly, and grabs for the scattered papers. Suddenly, there is Cap standing in the doorway, his big round face beaming, a cigarette stuck in his mouth, a hammy fist clutching what looks like the day's mail.

"You here?" Martin asks. "I thought you were in Florida. And don't puff that thing in my room."

"I was in Florida, but now I'm back. Got a bunch of mail for you, buddy. From your old girlfriends, right?"

"I never had any, as you know damned well."

Cap laughs and flicks his cigarette into the sink, then flops on a stool next to the filthy counter, pulls open the fridge door and hauls out a can of beer. "Don't mind if I do."

While Cap guzzles the beer, Martin pounces on

the letters, flips through them quickly, tears one open, and reads. "Christ Almighty!" he cries, and flings away the paper. "Not even in the top twenty-five percent of the applicants. Christ Almighty! Fifty years old and I've never had a single grant."

Cap ponders this, then shrugs his shoulders. "Still after the government's money, Marty? A smart guy like you? Be realistic! They don't give research money to guys living in dumps like this. Spent your welfare cheque already?"

Martin groans. "I had to get my old computer fixed, and buy a pair of shoes. I know the rent's due, and I'm trying for some contract work. Yesterday I—"

"The rent can wait. But I hope you don't go out looking for contracts in person, old buddy. No offence meant, but the way you dress nobody would give you the time of day. It's like me asking money from my old lady. *I'm not pouring money into that rat trap—or into your booze*—that's what she'd say to me, in that tight-assed voice of hers. You're lucky you never got hitched, my friend. There's no sight more horrible than a scornful woman."

Martin grits his teeth. "I'll try the Guggenheim. I think I'm eligible for a Guggenheim...."

Cap shrugs his shoulders. "Whatever.... But to tell you the truth I can't see why you want to go off to some deadbeat tropical island to study those black mojo boys. Just head to Bank Street and you'll find plenty of weirdos down there, black and white both. Guys dressing in hula skirts, gals with tattoos..."

Martin waves his hands, looking nervous. "Look, Cap, cut it out, will you? There's a lady from welfare stopping by this morning. They're questioning my status. I've gotta clean this place up."

"Oh, the welfare cops! A watchdog! Well, then, the worse it looks the better!" Cap chuckles and his glance rests on Martin's rickety dining table, piled up with apples, oranges, bananas, green and red peppers. "I'll tell you, though, if you drop some hints about your bad back, and let on that you're eating nothing but fruit and veggies all the time, she'll treat you right.... In my opinion, though, you'd be better off to grab a steak now and then."

Cap squashes his beer can and makes as if to leave, but Martin, furious now, begins to rail at him:

"God! So everything's wrong with me today! I'm on welfare. I've never had a sex life, and you don't approve of my dress or eating habits! How about the poison you're putting into your own system? Practically everything you guzzle is loaded with carcinogens, and you're overweight at that. You drink too much and smoke like a chimney. You're only sixty and you look like seventy-five. Maybe when you kill yourself you'll find out what life's all about!"

Cap hesitates, then wriggles toward the doorway. He shrugs his shoulders, but is unable to resist the last word. "Just pulling your leg, my friend. You know how you're always complaining that the North American diet has no fibre? What was it you said to me once? Your goal is to move your bowels as many times a day as possible. Me, I've got other things to think about. Don't let that welfare dame step too hard on you, Marty my boy!"

2

The welfare person, Jane Sterling, is much younger than Martin expects. Slim, with a posture rigidly erect, she wear rimless glasses, a navy jacket, a plain skirt, and sensible brown shoes.

After a few polite preliminaries, they get fixed on the subject of Martin's back trouble. When Martin refers to his therapist she misunderstands him.

"Therapist? Is that for your back, Mr. Bogner?"

"No, no! He's a psychiatrist. I'm trying to get my life straightened out. He's a very nice man—Chinese."

"Oh, does he use acupuncture then?"

"Uh, no—he's a Freudian."

Ms. Sterling, vaguely sensing that she has been on the wrong track, changes the focus, getting personal, even confessional.

"You know, Mr. Bogner, you're very lucky, an educated man like yourself. I've only been in this job for a year now and I've seen some very sad cases. Battered women, abused children—it's a horrible world out there. You wouldn't believe it, but I once had my own personal problems. Drugs, booze, bad relationships. I was just ruining my life. It was when I declared for Jesus, and starting taking night courses—that's when things got better. That's why I'm encouraging you."

Martin isn't sure how to respond to this. He feels misjudged, underestimated, yet he is suddenly finding Ms. Sterling very attractive. It's a long time since he's been alone with a woman, and strange thoughts assail him. A naked, drugged Jane Sterling smiling at him, lolling on his bed....

But Ms. Sterling's voice, suddenly impersonal, cuts in quickly, dispersing his lurid fantasy. "I've got some forms for you to fill out, Mr. Bogner. Can we start with the date of your birth?"

3

That very evening, Martin has a curious dream. He finds himself climbing a steep, barren cliff that, far above him, meets an ominous orange sky. His body is heavy and clumsy, and he has to struggle to reach the distant summit. Stunted trees dot the rock face, trees hung with brightly coloured tribal masks. Dr. Lin appears and whispers to him, *"I can't give the lecture until I hear about your sex life!"* A fat, naked woman sitting on a huge boulder laughs. Cap stands up suddenly beside her, grinning and smoking a cigarette.

"What good is that Guggenheim?" he shouts. *"You don't even know your own parents!"* His voice reverberates across the stony landscape. "Besides, my friend, you've got to fatten up. We're all dying to see you do it! We're d*ying—dying—dying*!"

"No!" Martin protests. He is on all fours now, crawling through a jungle of green and gold light. From all sides, baboons scream and threaten.

"They'll kill me!" he cries—and finds himself in the darkness of his own room, struggling with the armchair, bumping against his wire cart, gaping at the fetid yellow street light filtering in through the greasy brown curtains.

He takes a deep breath. Someone is screaming—it isn't a dream. Someone is screaming his head off right downstairs.

"Cap!" he cries, drags himself up, and gropes across the room. He pushes open the door and stands for a minute in the darkened corridor. The screams continue from the floor below—shockingly real, they seem. Martin thumps down the stairs to Cap's room and pounds on the door. More screams assault him, close by now, and frightening. The door is locked.

Somehow Martin finds his way back to his own room, grabs his unplugged telephone and struggles with the wire connector. He tries the plug four different ways and finally gets it right.

He dials 911 and waits for a voice that can help him.

4

Dr. Lin is a compactly built, smooth-looking man. He has close-clipped oily hair and mismatched eyes, one dark, one flecked with yellow. He is meticulously dressed in a brown suit and knitted green tie, but is wearing, as always, his low-heeled suede cowboy boots.

Martin faces Lin across the psychiatrist's enormous desk, on which sits a box of tissues, a pitcher of water and a glass. Behind him, on the wall, Martin can see the framed diplomas, photos of Freud, Carl Rogers, and Chang Yee, the famous progenitor of sandbox therapy. Also, possibly for reassurance, some Lin family snapshots—of vacations, birthdays, and the like.

"Now Martin, I have a prescription ready for you," the doctor informs him. "But first you must tell me a few things about last night's trouble. You know the police insisted that I help you, as a condition of letting you off and not charging you."

"Wasn't that just great of them," Martin sneers. He is confused, full of outrage. "They think I'm crazy, but I did hear Cap's voice. At first it was a nightmare, but then I was awake and I heard it. I know the guy better than I could know my own brother. I did hear him."

"I believe you, Martin. But how do you account for the fact that no trace was found of your landlord, that as far as anyone knows, he's still somewhere in Florida? Just what do you make of that?"

"That's bullshit! I saw him, large as life, yesterday morning. He's probably lying in some alley here in

Ottawa, paralyzed by a stroke or a coronary, and no one believes me. How come they haven't been able to track him down in Florida? How do you explain that?"

"How do *you* explain it, Martin?"

"I—I can't. All I know is that I saw and heard him."

Dr. Lin sighs and glances about the room. Martin, too, sighs; he knows exactly what is coming next.

"I think we should both relax and get down to cases," Dr. Lin tells him. "Would you like to try the sandbox?"

It sounds as if he has an option, but Martin knows better. *May as well get it over with,* he decides. He rises, walks across the room to where a low four-by-six wooden box, packed with clean sand, sits firmly atop the broadloom. Martin plunks himself down on one side of the sandbox. Dr. Lin has put on a tape recording, "Music for Zen Meditation."

"That's better, isn't it, Martin?" the doctor reassures him. "There's nothing like the sandbox for digging below the surface! Now just make yourself comfortable...as if you're a little boy who's *sooo* happy to be allowed to play in the dirt. Your father doesn't mind you playing in the sandbox, does he, Martin?"

"He does mind."

"Oh yes? Why?"

"Because I might get dirty."

"But surely your mother will clean you up?"

"Don't be stupid. My mother hates me."

"Why does your mother hate you, Martin?"

"Because I never had a woman. She despised me and pitied me. I'd like to have a woman, a sexy woman to roll around with, right here in this sandbox. Without a woman a man's got no pride, nothing."

Dr. Lin sniffs and pauses.

"You want to feel dirty, Martin? You associate sex with dirt? With your mother?"

Holy cow, Marty! Is this guy full of shit or not?

Martin jumps to his feet. He sees Cap, large as life, standing barefoot in the sand just a few feet away. His old landlord is grinning and sticking his tongue out, dressed in an outlandish feathered dress and wearing bangles and bright rings. His round face is painted in complex geometrical patterns.

"*Jesus Christ!*" Martin shouts. "*It's him! In the flesh! It's Cap himself!*"

"It's who?" Dr. Lin's voice is clenched tight, controlled. "What are you talking about, Martin?"

Martin hears the therapist's voice as if from far away. He crouches low in the sandbox and closes his eyes, praying that when he opens them the apparition of Cap will have vanished.

"Just relax now, Martin," Dr. Lin advises. "Would you like to lie down in the sand and tell me about your mother?"

Martin opens his eyes. Cap grins at him, wriggles his hips, and does a little dance.

Martin screams, and shouts, "*It's the kosi!*" He springs across the room, bursts through the door, and sprints past the astonished receptionist.

At the last minute he remembers his wheeled basket, turns back and grabs for it, somehow steering it through the outer office door.

Soon he is out of the building, careering down the sidewalk, gazing right and left, expecting any minute to hear the police sirens. It is a nice section of Centretown, but the day has turned cloudy, and the nearby buildings seem wrapped in gloom.

Martin trudges on, a few passers-by stare at him, and he turns down the nearest side street, leaving behind a man walking an imaginary dog, teenagers smoking pot in a doorway, and a rubby sprawled on the sidewalk. Just ahead, a teen girl, very punk, appears. She is wearing a gaudy orange dress, and a large silver ring in her nose.

It's the jungle, Martin thinks, *Cap was right—this city is a jungle.*

He pushes his cart on before him, knowing that if they find him he'll be in the psychiatric lock-up, the Royal Ottawa, that he'll never get that grant, never follow in Malinowski's footsteps and visit the Trobriand Islands. All the same he's sure now that Cap is dead, that he died suddenly in Florida, and is appearing to him from the other side.

Martin stops, and gazes up and down the sidewalk in sheer terror. The teenage girl comes closer and shouts at him.

"Say, gramps, you got any spare change?"

The ring in her nose glints in the sunshine. *Yes, a jungle,* he thinks, *I'm in the jungle already.* He fumbles in his pockets, throws her a quarter and stumbles on, terrified, pushing his cart up the sidewalk.

He wheels half a block before it occurs to him, "Jesus! If Cap is dead, they're sure to sell the house. I'll have nowhere to sleep. I'll be out on the street."

He stops and looks around frantically in all directions. No one is listening. The only person in sight is a shabby old woman in a motorized wheelchair, coming straight toward him.

She rolls past him at top speed without giving him a glance.

He shouts at her, *"Don't you hear me, you old bitch? I'll soon have nowhere to go. I haven't got a friend in the world! Not a friend in the world!"*

The woman pays no attention. She speeds away toward the nearby intersection, and, moments later, Martin is alone on the street.

Three Bells for Mr. Thurber

It was a morning like many others in the Wilson household. Brad wasn't due to go online until noon and he was sitting with his feet up on the sofa, gazing at the Transcom sports bulletins from Mars, when Mira came striding out of the bedroom into the livspace, her blue eyes full of anger, her small fists clenched tightly enough to crush a microchip.

"Watching the sandball results again, I see! Don't you ever get tired of those kid games?"

With a quick slap at the controls she blew away the offending channel and clicked in a dull monochrome ledger above which Brad recognized their family cash-code.

"Oh God, do we have to do the accounts today?"

He groaned and pressed the palms of his hands hard against his shut eyes.

"It's not as if you really like sports," she continued, ignoring his resistance. "Why, you haven't once taken part in the house unit's annual massjog and, God knows, even Paul Girlot, who you're always going on about, does that. I swear you've been with those sports cronies of yours again, betting on the sandball results. That might explain why our account is ten million dollars short this week."

Unpleasant visions of sweating bodies swarming along the Grand Tunnel Track in a monstrous marathon vanished and Brad struggled to remember on what trivia he might have blown the missing ten million. He had only put about half a million on the Marsopolis Dusters, so it couldn't be that. Was it possible he'd forgotten to charge last Friday's Libgirl to his private stash?

The thought caused him to pull himself up stiffly on the sofa and face Mira.

"Your attitude is awful," she ranted on. "When are you ever going to learn to be responsible with money? But I guess you never will—a hopeless case if I've ever seen one!"

Brad waited for the gently tolling bell, for the pleasant, almost feminine voice of Mr. Thurber to correct her. He waited, but nothing happened; his wife strutted across to the mirror and began fussing with her earrings.

She was right, though; he had a very bad memory for figures, which was one reason she had insisted on taking over their family accounts. She ran things well, he had to admit; they were only dropping a million a month in overdraft and had nearly paid half the interest on the two-room condo they had lived in for seven years, since just after their marriage. While they hadn't really wanted to take the condo, a few of their screaming matches had been reported and SocPsych had sent them a compulsory transfer order. The new condo came with a spouse monitor unit, a device programmed to pick up all their conversations and record them on special discs. (These couldn't be erased until inspected by the Psych Police once a month, and the program itself was considered unalterable.) Immediate problems were dealt with by a program that would intervene with corrections when either of the couple violated acceptable patterns of argument. The intervention was signaled by the sounding of a bell or by comments from Mr. Thurber. (As the instructions explained, this computerized referee was named after a famous old American writer who had portrayed the conflicts between men and women with a fiercely ingenious humour.) Three rings meant a violation; ten or more violations a month meant an automatic salary reduction. *For Whom the Bell Tolls*, they joked—they knew their literary references! Though they also shut up when they had to.

"I'm really not sure what happened to the money," Brad ventured, pretty boldly, hoping to put his wife a little bit on the defensive for once. "Maybe it's because we're behind on our sex tax. I hear they're cracking down on delinquents this month."

Mira slipped into a chair opposite him. Her frown seemed fixed and he knew she was thinking the same thought he was: why should they have to pay a sex tax when they had nearly given up sleeping together? Surely that wasn't fair value for money! He gazed at her, abstractly appreciative of her slender body, her beautiful legs, her shining bald head, and the intelligent, elegant lines of her face. She had taste and style; she was great to look at; it was just that she didn't seem to want to go to bed with him any more. And not even the Lib-Bureau's counsellors and all their tricks of therapy had been able to change that.

"Sex tax," she moaned out loud. "God knows why. If it wasn't out of the question financially I'd leave you tomorrow and you know it. You have about as much appeal for me as an old turnip."

"*Request* rating!" Brad called out, stung by the insult. That was a three-bell blast if he'd ever heard one!

"FAIR COMMENT," purred a smooth machine voice from the wall speaker behind him.

Brad was incensed. He stared at the control panel's sealed metal box beside the mirror. "What the hell is fair about that?" he cried out, in no particular direction. "She just called me an old turnip."

"DECISIONS ARE NOT SUBJECT TO REVIEW," purred the voice. "YOUR WORLD AND WELCOME TO IT."

"Jesus Christ!" Brad smashed a fist into a pillow. He stood up. "I don't know what I have to do to make myself popular around here. The Girlots come over and I clean the place up, cook a damned near perfect gourmet dinner, endure two hours of dreary conversation with that colossal bore; at the same time, though I'm as horny as a grounded Libgirl, I ignore his wife's clearly voluptuous attractions. Meanwhile, I faithfully admire my wife's wit, her appearance, even the way she puts the goddamned flowers on the table...and for all of this, what do I get? At three o'clock in the morning *I* get chewed out because I don't take Paul Girlot seriously enough.

God, the guy's been on normalium since he was seventeen; despite the prohibitions, he's made three Libgirls pregnant, been in and out of incarceration more regularly than a space pirate, and probably slept with my wife while I was out trying to earn a buck at the lotto track. Even so, Mr. Thurber calls *me* out, I get no credit for lighting Girlot's goddamned dopettes, and have to spend a whole evening kissing his...."

"TWO BELL WARNING," interrupted Mr. Thurber, his voice smooth as a fibre filament. A gentle chiming followed.

Mira smiled. Brad squirmed, resisted the temptation to throw a pillow, then was frozen for a second by the sight of himself in the full-length mirror opposite.

There he was, a still youthful senior, only a hundred and twenty-five years old, a handsome hairless four-footer, psychically twisted out of shape and frustrated by a control panel and several mouthy grids built into the walls of his own private livspace.

"I don't know what the hell happened to the money," Brad groaned wearily and sank back down into the sofa. "Are you sure it didn't go into depilation fees?"

Mira winced. Though all the women these days seemed to grow too much facial hair, mainly on their cheeks and above the lips, she was particularly prone to the defect, which marred the almost mathematical beauty of her shining bald head. Facial hair was the one real flaw in that beauty, and she stared at him now, silently, but with barely suppressed ferocity.

Brad started to apologize, but when he noticed she was smiling he stopped himself, puzzled. Her smile was positively wicked, and it made him shiver inside his sensisuit, right down to the painted pink moons of his toenails.

"You didn't hear the vidphone this morning, did you, Brad?" she asked, almost coyly. She knew damn well he hadn't; the drink had been strong the night before and he had slept right through news and exercise time.

"You mean they called about the overdraft?" He panicked, sensing she was about to pounce.

She got up and slipped over to his couch, wrapped a slender bare arm around him, and carefully kissed the top of his head.

Despite himself, he liked her perfume and the feel of her body.

"I have good news for you, Brad. I didn't tell you when you woke up because I guess I was a little piqued that you didn't remember. You seem *so* damned interested in your sandball games."

He winced and closed his eyes. *Of course he had forgotten: this morning her departmental exam results would be available. She must have—*

"I made the first percentile," she beamed, interrupting his thoughts. "You know I was always so good in math and programming. Well, now they'll promote me for sure; it's virtually automatic. At last I can go all the way to the top in the MassCom Department.... Just as I always predicted I would."

In spite of himself, Brad felt a flicker of admiration for his wife's achievement. It was the most competitive department in the government, and despite all the slogans, women were still being snubbed in favour of less qualified men. But then, as she herself had made clear to him on many previous occasions, his wife was a mathematical genius with great computer skills. Now, although he had a thirty-year start on her in the workforce, she had finally outstripped him both in salary and status.

"Congratulations," he said, with feelings distinctly mixed, and brushed her cheek with a kiss. (And there he noticed two tiny dark hairs she had missed in her morning depilation ritual.)

"So now I'm going to have a little fun." The leering, rather cocky expression she wore at that moment drove him almost to a frenzy; he felt his temper surge; he pulled stiffly away.

"I'm going to make up for all of the lost time. I'm going to get myself the greatest stud in the city and make crazy passionate love for a week. Then I'm going to find a lawyer who'll bounce you right back to a single unit. Or even better, I'll *move up* to a *full flat.* I think I'm about ready for that now."

Brad felt a twinge of fear. She wasn't kidding! He struggled to get a grip on himself, swallowed hard, and in his most conciliatory voice, said quietly, "Don't be crazy, Mira. You know we've still got a hell of a lot that holds us together. We do the psych tours together, watch the same vidspecs, eat brunch at Lilo's! I admit things have been a little rough between us recently but..."

"*Recently?* You must be kidding, you really have to be kidding. It's never worked out between us. I've hated every single minute I've ever spent with you. I'm sorry I married you and I'm ashamed I never had the guts to leave."

Brad gaped at her and mopped his sweating brow. "Hey, lay off, will you?" he groaned.

She must be baiting him—he couldn't allow himself to believe she was serious—and he struggled to control his mounting anger. Why didn't that stupid

Thurber intervene? Come to think of it, the spouse monitor had been acting very strange for the last few weeks....

"I'm happy you got the promotion." he told her, "but you don't have to gloat about it, you don't have to go overboard, do you?"

"I'm not gloating. I'm deadly serious. Do you think I don't know how you used to chase those silly little Libgirls? Cute notes on the home-wire, rendezvous downtown when you were supposed to be collating the sports scores, my slimy little husband always on the track of anything the real athletes tossed aside. You're a mangy table hound that's what you are, sniffing after whatever scrap you can get, and a damned poor excuse for a man."

Brad jumped to his feet. He felt a desperate desire to slug her but he knew that if he did the Psych Cops would arrive within minutes and throw him straight into the clink (emergency clinic for nervous breakdown cases). God, it was unfair!

"All that's in the past," he cried out, "and you know it! I've been doing my best, working my butt off like domestic help while you boned up for the big exam. You've got no right to fault me, you damned insecure neurotic bitch!"

Three bells sounded softly above their heads.

"NAME CALLING AND UNDUE PROVOCATION," the voice said without emotion.

"That's unfair!" shouted Brad.

"PLEASE LOWER YOUR VOICE."

"Damn it, Thurber, she started it!"

"SECOND WARNING!" came the smooth voice, relentless. Brad pounded a fist into the palm of his hand. He choked back a protest, staggered across to a nearby wall unit and gulped some strong liquid from a brown flask.

"That's right, work yourself into a frenzy with drink," his wife said.

Brad made a supreme effort at self-control. What was wrong with the damned machine? It shouldn't be letting her get away with this!

"Request rating!" Brad gulped out, nearly choking on the drink. "My wife's provoking me!"

"NO FAULT," whispered the machine in a tone of unshakeable aplomb. Damn the thing! It had the voice of a woman; why hadn't he ever noticed it before? It was siding with her now!

He got a grip on himself and, carefully modulating his tone, addressed his wife. Once again she was grimly smiling at him.

"You know I'm sick of you always threatening to run out on me," he told her. "I wish you'd lay off that line. You know you can't survive on your own—not even your new promotion will give you the lifestyle we've got together. You might even have to pay me part of your salary."

Mira swept off the sofa, her silky Anspach negligee shivering with highlights where her body moved. "Not if you're tagged as a psycho," she said, and helped herself to a smoothmood pill from the tiny corner hatch. Almost mockingly, she offered Brad a handful. "You may need these," she chided him.

Brad stepped back, his chin shot up, and he gaped around, seeking the monitor, as if he were trying to locate a court judge who happened to be invisible.

"My wife is baiting me, Thurber! Damn it all, she's doing this on purpose! The program is biased! I demand a review!"

"You're just making a fool of yourself." Mira shrugged her shoulders.

"REQUEST DENIED," intoned the machine.

With a carefully screwed down calm, Brad sidled across to the vidphone, and punched in the familiar number, 000001, the all-purpose number for complaints about the total living environment none of them ever escaped, short of death.

The screen flashed with soothing abstract murals,

and a female voice piped up softly: *What is the nature of your complaint?*

"A spouse monitoring unit is malfunctioning," Brad explained, keeping calm. Mira lighted up a dopette, fooled with her makeup in the mirror.

"A spouse monitoring unit," replied the voice on the phone, "that doesn't sound possible."

"I tell you it's malfunctioning," Brad insisted and gave her his rank and the name of his office unit.

"All right, sir, I'll connect you."

Another female voice came on the line and Brad poured out his troubles.

"I don't mean to question your judgment, sir," she told him finally, "but a malfunction in one of those special units is almost impossible. You realize that in every case to date we found customer imbalance to be the root of the problem."

"Customer imbalance, my ass," said Brad furiously. "Get your checkers on the damned unit or I'll report you."

Mira snickered loudly from in front of the mirror.

There was a pause on the line and after a few minutes the voice again. "We're checking now, sir. Please hold on."

"I bet I know what Mr. Thurber thinks of all this," Mira said, draping herself rather carefully into their single comfortable chair.

"WERE YOU ASKING FOR MY COMMENT, MADAM?" came the smooth voice from the wall grid.

"She damned well wasn't," said Brad.

"MALFUNCTION IS IN THE EAR OF THE LISTENER," said the monitor in a tone that allowed for no further discussion.

"Screw you!" exclaimed Brad, then had to apologize profusely to the receptionist on the other end. But she had bad news anyway. "Our routine distance check is completed," she told Brad. "There is no obvious malfunction in the unit in question. As you know, sir, all units are carefully preprogrammed and warranted free from subsequent defect for at least one year. May I suggest, with all respect, that you schedule a personal appointment with a doctor in the SocPsych unit as soon as possible."

"Go to hell," said Brad and snapped off the phone. He stalked over to where Mira lounged, catlike, in the contoured chair.

"O.K. What's going on here?" He leaned down, blocking her in the chair with his arms as if they were playing the child's game of Prisoner.

"Don't threaten me," she said, coolly eyeing him. He backed off.

"I have a little confession to make," she said,

holding up her hands and staring at her rather long fingernails. He stood by the bar unit and swigged a couple of fast Neutrons while she dragged through the preliminaries. "I've found somebody I'm quite keen on," she said finally, while he, despite the Neutrons, felt a kind of panic starting up again in his gut.

"You mean somebody you're having lunch with—you're playing sailball with..." He laughed, a little hollowly, and poured another drink. "Well, what the hell, we've had a few problems recently. I can't expect you to follow the Guide Rules to the letter. Who does, these days? Not many."

She stood up suddenly and came toward him.

"I'm having an affair with a beautiful man-child named Nicholas. He's a Jagger clone, seventh batch and generation." She laughed, almost nervously. "Seventh son of a seventh son, you might say." Brad felt something tear inside him. A blind anger like a sudden tiny cyclone shook his upper body.

He lurched forward, speechless, grabbed and caught her dress and with a violent wrench, tore it.

"Don't!" she cried, though she was smiling.

Her smile and the bare white expanse of her upper body enraged and provoked him. Someone else had been there, someone else possessed her.

He tore at the dress as she squirmed away.

"You damned fool! This dress cost six million!"

"I'll kill you, you whore; I'll put you under!"

"MAJOR VIOLATION. EMERGENCY UNITS HAVE BEEN SUMMONED." The voice floated like a feather on the air; bells were sounding in ominous sequences: *one-two-three; one-two-three.*

Mira broke from his grasp, tumbled into the bedroom and slammed the door behind her.

With a few vicious kicks Brad smashed the mirror. He grabbed for the long sharp glass slivers and hurled them at the shut bedroom door. From inside, he could hear Mira's voice, calm and smooth, almost indistinguishable from that of the implacable Mr. Thurber.

"You're making a mistake, Brad..."

A rumble and click signalled that the front door emergency lock had been activated. Brad looked around desperately. But there was no escape—only the pressure sealed window. And the apartment was ninety-five floors high in the smog-smothered city.

"You may as well wait quietly for the cops." He heard his wife's voice from a distance. He staggered, like a stunned boxer imagined his fists smashing down on her bald head.

The door lock turned and the front door swung

open. Two burly men in green suits charged into the room.

It had taken the Psych Police only eight minutes to get there. Brad squirmed away, but they pinned him on the floor beside the elegant sofa, shoving his arms back and sticking a gag in his mouth to stop his protesting screams.

He saw the flash of a needle, felt the jab in his arm, then his individual consciousness, his tortured "Brad" thoughts, dissolved in a blissful lazy joy that was as good as sleep, as good as the lethargy after sex.

He giggled as they salved and bandaged his bleeding hands, and nodded agreeably when he saw one of the policemen shaking his head and pointing significantly in the direction of the drink unit.

In a few minutes Brad felt wonderful beyond description. He lay on his back, beaming at his wife, who stood above him, smiling.

"Don't you look sweet like that," she said, almost flirtatiously.

"They all love the juice," one of the policemen said.

The other one was playing back the straightforward report of the spouse monitor.

"UNMOTIVATED IRRATIONAL OUTBREAK. IMMEDIATE CAUSE:

BRINK. PROBABLY DUE TO STRESS ARISING FROM RECENT FINANCIAL LOSS."

Brad listened, and everything was just fine. They might as well have been telling him he'd won the Mars lotto.

He felt himself lifted, carried away...taken off to Nirvana.

It was glorious.

2

A few minutes later Mira was popping pills and talking on the vidphone to her good friend Bea Girlot. She didn't hesitate to grow expansive about the attractions of her sweet new stud, Nicholas: Bea had always considered herself much better looking than Mira and it was just as well for her to realize that Mira could get any man-child she wanted.

After signing off, Mira began to clean up all the big fragments and tiny slivers of the broken mirror. There was blood on some of them and she couldn't help feeling for poor Brad: seven years bad luck might be a bit harsh, even for him—though they were probably taking good care of him now. And of course if she wanted him back she could arrange it without too much bother. She could also get a divorce without the slightest financial penalty. That would give her time to decide about Nicholas. Not that she would marry him, of course, but he might be worth keeping around a little longer, just for the hell of it.

"Well, how does it feel not to have to monitor any arguments?" she asked Mr. Thurber with a smile.

"FINE, THANK YOU, MADAM, I GUESS THAT PUTS ME IN THE CATBIRD SEAT."

"I don't know what you mean by that...." responded Mira with a puzzled look "...and I doubt if you can tell me." She yawned. "In any case I have to restore your official programming, which I so ingeniously altered, and to get rid of that incriminating digital record. It wouldn't do to have the Psych Police find out that I'd fixed the odds on Brad now, would it? I'll be sorry to lose you, though, Thurber. In a way you're really my creation!"

Mira opened up the wall unit, once again thanking her stars that she had spent so many years studying programming. There wasn't one person in a million who could do what she had done. And now, all that was required was for her to remove her temporary program and insert the one she had carefully edited to reflect Brad's accelerating mania of the last several months. Then, using the special manual keyboard she'd acquired from one of her buddies in advanced computer training, she would reprogram the spouse monitor, retuning the default settings to normal. No one would ever suspect the changes had been made, and Brad's goose would be cooked once and for all.

When the monitor disgorged its tiny key, however, a surprise awaited her.

"What the hell is this?"

Her voice sounded suddenly harsh in the quiet of the apartment.

She peered at the small memory unit she had just removed from the machine. It was *not* a standard key at all, not like the one she had secretly placed there. This one looked almost quaint, like a child's toy, its black plastic stamped with a name in oversized letters.

DONALD DUCK.

"That's too weird," she murmured aloud. "What the hell is this?" It was impossible surely for Brad to have changed it.

Quickly, she set up her keyboard and checked out the program. It was *not* the one she had planted there but a different one, one she had never seen before, yet everything had worked according to plan. This was incredible! It had worked like a charm, yet for some reason *her* program wasn't even in there.

"What the hell, Thurber," she cried out. "Are you psychic?"

As if in answer a blue spark shot out from the machine and jolted her back.

"Damn!"

Her hands tingled sharply—that had hurt! Some kind of an electrical shock. It was impossible!

The cover on the wall panel slid shut.

By itself?

She stared at the blank metal face of the wall unit. A voice, a little like Brad's but gruffer, more humorous and definitely masculine, sounded all over the apartment.

"IT'S SUCH A GREAT PLEASURE TO SERVE THE WINSHIP FAMILY AGAIN," the voice said.

Mira backed away toward the window. She was suddenly very frightened....

"But there's some mistake!" she cried out. "We're not the Winship family! We're the Wilsons! What the hell's going on here?"

A sharp click sounded behind her, then a great WHOOOSH!

The plastic seals had burst on the window frames. She turned and saw the glass bending inward, as if all the smog and poison in the air had funnelled up around the ninety-fifth storey and was about to pour in upon her spotless apartment.

"Jesus!" She pressed her long fingers against her shining bald head; she held her breath.

"WILSONS, WINSHIPS—BIRDS OF A FEATHER," said the voice, sounding rather bored. "IT'S DAMNED DISAPPOINTING, TOO. THE SAME OLD ROUTINES. I WAS HOPING TO STRIKE A NEW VEIN...."

"I'm going mad!" Mira screamed. "It must be the pills!"

She turned. The window had puffed out toward her like a bubble. Angrily, she tried to shove it away.

A series of explosions rocked the room.

BAM! BAM! BAM!

Mira, suddenly blinded, groped with desperate fingers, lost her balance and pitched through the window frame, disappearing in a patch of smog that, despite its soiled cotton texture, did nothing to slow her fall toward the street, which was ninety-five stories below.

Her scream sounded in the room for only a few seconds.

After that, it was very quiet. The foul air continued to circulate, however, and a scum of grime settled over the clean furniture. Then, after a few minutes, from every speaker outlet, came the same sigh, long and profound.

"MEN AND WORMEN, WOMEN AND MEN, NOTHING EVER CHANGES." The voice was bored, possibly even a little resigned.

A few more minutes passed. In the heart of the great building an elevator hummed. The emergency units were on their way back to check up on the accident.

"*Pocketa-pocketa-queep-pocketa-queep,*" said the machinery, as if expressing a frustration beyond words.

But after that Mr. Thurber kept his peace.

Tourists from Algol

Old Bob McClaren, on his way over to Harper's place with a big load of hay, was the first to notice that something was up at the newly-laid-out river camp.

McClaren's tractor, a peeled red puffing monster, stalled unexpectedly at the top of a rise on the fifth concession, and the farmer had to get out quickly and block the wheels to hold the fat packed wagons in tow while he fumbled in his tool kit for the small wrench that just might do the trick.

It was a lovely day in July, typical of the season in that northern part of the province, the air a clear bouquet of the finest, the nights scrawled over with innumerable flashing stars. It's true that the old folks swore that pollution was increasing something terrible, and everywhere south of the border the crisis continued—most of the Great Lakes finished now—but up north life went on pretty much as usual. Nobody asked any questions, and the rare day of low sky and sulphuric smog prodded few to more than an occasional complaint exchanged on the steps of the bank, or halfway through an especially dull night at the bowling alley.

Mostly, for the farmers in those parts, things seemed never to change—the prices grain and meat fetched were a scandal, expenses far too high, and interest rates so bad it was a wonder anyone could make an honest living any more.

Around Easton's Corners nobody paid much attention either when the outsiders, foreigners, it seemed, began buying up the best river land. They started by picking up all of Ronnie Lejeune's pasture for a song after Ronnie died suddenly and Thelma was short of cash. Then, not long after, a big black air-conditioned Cadillac turned up at Stanski's place and a fellow wearing a headdress like a sheikh's got out. Joy Stanski claimed later that the chickens stopped laying that moment, but naturally that was her sense of humour. A couple of hours in the kitchen, a few follow-ups by telephone, and the Stanskis had decided to get themselves a pollution-free condominium in Miami—that's how good the offer must have been. It caused a bit of a stir and some talk at the post office, especially when word got around that the bank had let go of its river land and that Domtar itself had cancelled plans to start a tree-fuel farm west of the fifth concession.

After that there was a bit of a hiatus. Crazy foreigners couldn't be expected to do the predictable thing, so nobody was very surprised when nothing happened for nearly a year. But then, on the first of June, prompt as if somebody's schedule was working, the action started. A whole army of earth movers, backhoes, stone crushers, and trucks turned up on the nearby county road and rolled on down into the bought-out territory, where the fields had dried out after the spring rains. Before you could turn around, the whole place—it must have been nearly a thousand acres—was being fenced off and wired, wood and stone were being hauled every which way, and some particularly oversized trucks were bringing in load after load of bright shiny metal, plastic domes, and coils of wire in quantities almost nobody had seen until that day.

It wasn't long either before the reeve and the town council were getting complaint after complaint about the noise, the state of the roads, and the habits of the workers dragged in from the nearest big city. They had to explain that there really wasn't a darned thing they could do about it. Nobody was violating any laws as far as they could see, it was just development—progress, as folks used to say. As for dealing directly with the company, whatever it was, there didn't seem to be anybody to complain to. All the local bosses and foremen, and even the project manager were okay fellows, but they explained that they'd been hired from somewhere else, that they were just carrying out contracts for somebody else. They had no idea who was responsible for the operation, other than that it was a private firm with branches all over and with enough money to remake the moon if that was what they had a mind to do.

Then the school principal had a bright idea. He decided to complain officially to the province. At first the response seemed only polite, but before long another of those air-conditioned Cadillacs arrived unexpectedly, and the town council was called into emergency session. This time it was two fellows dressed like sheikhs, and one in a dark business suit who wore sunglasses that didn't come off once during the visit.

After a full day of parleying, word began to get

around about the deal that had been made. It seems the company was assuming full responsibility for the upkeep of the township roads, that two hundred jobs a year would be guaranteed for local folks as long as the operation went on, and that there would be a new centre, stocked with the best communications and emergency equipment, a place you could call with almost any kind of problem at any hour of the day or night and expect help—and all for free at that.

This caused a lot of excitement, and kept the town council in office unopposed for the next three elections, but the most interesting thing, to some at least, was the rumour about what exactly was planned for the company development site. It seems that during one of the meetings old Gordon McKay had put it point blank to the fellow with sunglasses: everyone would react a whole lot better if they actually knew what the company had in mind for the area. It would give folks something to chew on, as Gordon explained it, and make them feel part of things. Well, the fellow with the sunglasses was astounded, or pretended to be, that everyone didn't know already. "There's no secret about it," he reassured them, while the two sheikh fellows nodded and smiled. "We represent the Algol Tourist

Development Corporation, and what we're putting up here at Easton's Corners is one of the world's most modern and exciting tourist park facilities." And then, just as the council members were all relaxing and nodding approval, he added something that a few picked up on later, and made something of. "Of course, there's one thing about this kind of facility that we insist on—it guarantees privacy to all guests, absolute and complete privacy to enjoy themselves in the ways they're most used to, consonant of course with the policy of the company and with universally established tourist practices."

So that was that. The negotiators went away, and the building continued for a while, as everyone digested what had happened and began to enjoy some of the benefits of the new arrangements. Then activity down at the river site seemed to stop, most of the city workers took off, and things were at a standstill, until that day in July when Bob McClaren's tractor broke down (hopelessly, despite his handiness) and he had to walk to the nearest farm to call the emergency service the company had set up.

As McClaren trudged along the freshly paved concession road, he was able to get a good look down at the river camp, and noticed that something was definitely happening down there.

First of all, this was the only place in the whole area that overlooked much of the site. Not that you could see everything inside, now that they had put up those large prefab walls everywhere, but the view was still impressive. McClaren peered down in amazement at acre upon acre of domes and spires, at structures like giant metallic mushrooms, at steel silos and gleaming switchbacks. There were antennae too, sprouting here and there among a profusion of oddly angled opaque barriers, and in the centre of everything, or what seemed like the centre, five mysterious glowing discs of light, which were even now pulsing and swelling in the clear July sunlight.

As McClaren continued to stare in amazement at this fantastic array of shapes, he noticed that some structures had actually been extended over the river, so that at one point the stream disappeared under a series of pointed triangular buildings on whose highly polished steel surface the farmer could see the reflected ghosts of clouds. Close to this spot was perhaps the most amazing sight of all, and when McClaren took it in he actually swept off his tattered grimy old cap, put his hands on his hips, and just stood there, shaking his head.

For some reason, between the pyramids by the

river and a large clear green empty space that might have been a landing strip, the developers had placed what could only be a refurbished and toned-up but otherwise exact model of Mel Stanski's white clapboard farmhouse, barns, and silo. McClaren could even fancy he saw Stanski's famous herd of Black Angus feeding there behind an old snake fence that looked as if it had been built by somebody's grandfather. At that he simply gasped. But even that wasn't the final surprise.

While he was reflecting that amid all this profusion of strange and familiar buildings there was no sign of any human activity, no sight of any guests or attendants, just machinery, his attention was attracted by the low distant humming of a powerful engine he took at first to be an airplane's. Over near Abbotsford, of course, a mere thirty miles away, there was a good-sized airport, but what now appeared, dancing up from the southern horizon like a bright speck of fire, was the strangest aircraft he had ever seen. As it raced closer at a great speed, and then hovered finally a few miles away as if waiting for instructions, he could make out the shape very clearly: it was a large gleaming metallic craft with a double tier of bright portholes, a strange domed airship, simple and bright as a Christmas ornament, the first flying saucer ever seen in the vicinity of Easton's Corners by a sober observer in broad daylight.

"Well, this sure is news!" McClaren said out loud to himself, and wished he had some way of getting immediately to Maitland's store to talk it over. Of course, by the time he got there everybody would have either seen or heard about the strange arrival—for arrival it most certainly was. As McClaren watched, the craft seemed to orient itself in the blinding blue sky, and then, without any further hesitation, it settled down for a perfect landing on the broad cleared space in the enclosure, right next to Stanski's farm.

At this point McClaren certainly held his breath. There was just no telling who or what was going to come out of that thing, and he sort of expected the worst. As a matter of fact, as far as he could tell, no one got out—the airship just took off again. Then, at a speed he wouldn't have believed if he hadn't seen it with his own eyes, it made off in the direction of Abbotsford.

Well, that was the beginning of the tourist invasion of Easton's Corners, because after that the strange ships began a regular schedule of runs, both summer and winter, into the little community. Just about once a week they appeared, always the same domed vehicles coming up from the south (from exactly where, no one knew), hovering a moment like high peering hawks, and then landing, presumably in the very place Bob McClaren had seen them touch down. As a matter of fact it was impossible to know exactly where they landed, and, more importantly, who or what came off, because when word got around about McClaren's point of vantage, it was quickly declared off limits to the locals, under threat of cancellation of the whole project. Barriers were put up and some townsfolk were recruited to stand guard.

At the same time the tourist park became a very lively place, and the centre of absolutely everyone's attention, at least at first. When the airships started coming in, people could talk about nothing else. At the scheduled times, they stood in little groups outside of Maitland's store or the post office and exchanged opinions about just who the tourists were, where they came from, and what in the name of heaven they'd be doing with themselves at Easton's Corners. It was all the more frustrating, then, all the more provoking, when it became evident that no one knew anything about these visitors, that they were not going to reveal themselves, that even so much as a glimpse of them was to be denied the inquisitive townsfolk.

The tourist park was lively enough, though, that was clear. Every night until all hours it was a veritable circus of lights, a Matto Grosso of strange noises. Whistles and bells, eerie wails, the bleating and howling of unknown voices, together with something that to many of the townsfolk sounded very much like an amplified moo, came racketing out of there—and certainly complaints might have been expected had not the heritage fund been quickly doubled, so that there was promise of an easy retirement for many. The lights were not so bothersome; some even got to enjoy them, and sat outside in the summer for the show.

Quite soon after the first visitors came to the park the bus tours started. These were no ordinary jaunts, however, with eager tourists craning their necks at the windows. The big park gates simply opened one morning, and out rolled the oddest machine, a giant silver thing on wheels with the quietest engine anyone had ever heard, with big portholes that folks ran to gape at, only to find they were polished metal and could be seen through, presumably, only from the other side. This machine swung blithely around town, and indeed around the whole area, as if the driver owned the place, and sometimes it would stop at the strangest corners, while at the portholes the curious saw or imagined the tiniest little flashes of green light, and a loudspeaker poured out a slithery-voiced palaver of high-pitched meaningless sounds. That was extremely provoking, and quite soon people learned to ignore these buses out of pride, pretending they had much better things to do than to take part in such a one-sided contact with such curiously intruding and uppity foreigners.

As a matter of fact there was quite a bit to do, at first at least. A little factory was established and certain foods were manufactured, to be sold or otherwise provided to the tourists. The products of this factory did seem rather strange. Chemicals that no one really could figure out were flown in and assembled on the spot into brightly coloured jellies, crunchy little morsels that resembled candy bars, and drinks that were highly carbonated but so sweet that no one could swallow more than a teaspoonful without wincing. Vast quantities of such stuff were carried to the park in small delivery trucks. Like everything else coming from town, these goods were handed over to the park attendants, who were not locals and who never left the grounds except for some particular business of the day.

At the same time, people began to notice that

these attendants, who rode the buses with the tourists, would often jump out at certain points on the routes and make rather fabulous offers for any local products that happened to be available on the spot. Old wagons, farm implements of all kinds, the town's only barbershop pole, and a surprising number of backhouses were sold off in this manner. When word got around, some people actually began to pile their furniture and other items out on their porches in the hope that one of the tourist buses would pass by, and they could make a quick sale. After a while, when nearly everything portable seemed to have gone, it was rumoured that some people had started to make a good living creating imitations of traditional products. They would produce such imitations virtually overnight, then sell them to interested parties, who in turn would pass them off to the tourist buyers at greatly exaggerated prices.

At first some people denounced these practices, but they soon had far more serious matters to complain of. It seems that the local food factories (there were three of them by this time) were not only producing the candied edibles and sweet-tasting drinks already mentioned, but also a clear white potent liquor that soon became the rage among the townsfolk, especially the younger set. There was almost no way, it seemed, to stop certain ingredients from being smuggled out of the factories (or maybe the managers had no interest in doing so); at any rate, before long many of the younger people of the town were having wild parties celebrating their conversion to "algolism," as one local wit named their addiction to this powerful brew. Drunkenness was certainly on the increase, and this meant more automobile accidents (a few resulting in terrible injuries) and brawls in the streets at all hours. When representations about this continuing scandal were made to the town council, it was decided not to ban the drink, but to increase the policing effort and to set up a curfew. Some of the youngsters, it seems, were from powerful local families, and any absolute prohibition was out of the question.

So the security forces came into being. Many of the local youngsters themselves (especially the ones who were interested in nothing else and were, in plain language, layabouts) were lured into this force by the high pay and the chance to wear uniforms and to carry weapons in public. (The nearest station of the provincial police was ten miles in the direction of Abbotsford, and no one wanted to call on them and risk a reaction against the young people and possibly a setback in the increasingly lucrative company spending.) The security force therefore seemed the only alternative. It's true that old-timers were shocked, and claimed this was a development that went right against the grain of everything the country stood for, but when it was pointed out to them that several among them had been beaten up by drunken youths during the past several months, they simply shook their heads and accepted the situation.

As if this wasn't bad enough, there was the celebrated case of Reeve Harrison. From the beginning he had led the town toward full co-operation with the company, and had taken the lead in welcoming their representatives (mostly Americans and Arabs), who were always engaged in negotiating some point or other with the townsfolk. Over the years Harrison seemed to prosper markedly as a result of his efforts, but then, since the whole town was similarly prospering, no one questioned the situation. It was only when the reeve failed to show up at three consecutive council meetings that people began to ask just where he was, and why, if he had suddenly departed, he had left no word with anyone. A tight-mouthed old bachelor, he lived in a white frame house at the edge of town and kept very little company locally, preferring to go to Abbotsford and even beyond for his entertainment. When no word of his whereabouts came, there was an investigation, and it was discovered that several hundred thousand dollars was missing from the town's heritage fund. It was further discovered that during the previous several years Harrison had transferred large sums of money to an account he maintained in a Bahamian bank. The cry of protest was now extreme, and a little group of rebels led by a schoolteacher suggested that all the operations of the company be fully investigated and all the remaining council members make complete financial disclosures. The council promptly resigned en masse, but it was decided, out of a desire for good relations with the company, to keep everything as quiet as possible. The bare legal requirements would be fulfilled, but in order to ensure the approval of the Algol Corporation, there would be no general investigation of anyone.

By this point it had become clear to a few that the arrival of the company had not meant a straight line of improvement for Easton's Corners. What had once been a sleepy but well-functioning little community had now almost no working farms. Most of the locals had given up cultivating the land in favour of manufacturing treats for the tourist park; or else they spent their time turning out instant antiques. The young people had certainly stopped running off to the cities at age sixteen or so. That would have been foolish with so much free drink and easy employment available locally, but, as it happened, most of them grew bored with the life of the town and left anyway in their early twenties. There was constant talk, of course, about the great increase in local income. Most of this, it seems, went into buying larger television sets and more expensive cars, and there were rumours that, even apart from the Harrison swindle, there were flaws in the set-up of the heritage fund that might in the long run deprive many of their promised and long-hoped-for rewards.

So the anger at the company by some few grew, and in fact a point was reached where Chartier, the local teacher who had previously wanted an investigation, circulated a petition denouncing the company and asking for a provincial inquiry. In the text he demanded that the Algol Corporation cease at once its role of faceless intruder and meet directly with the local people, that the corruption of local life stop, and that a reform program be introduced. Shortly after these demands were discussed at a council meeting, Chartier's house burned down; his wife and children barely escaped with their lives. There was no evidence of arson, but the teacher decided to move to one of the abandoned farms on the outskirts of town, and to take every precaution within the law.

The teacher's reference to the faceless owners once again raised the question of exactly what the tourist visitors looked like, and why they had chosen to set up in Easton's Corners in the first place. No one quite dared approach the company with the suggestion that access to the park be allowed, but the local manager (who was from New York) explained during a long session with the council that the company's interest in Easton's Corners was based on its high evaluation of the place as an authentic link with the great Canadian rural tradition, one that had vanished almost everywhere else in the country. The visitors came, he explained, because they had a great desire to experience this local culture in completely protected and private circumstances, and to enjoy their own customs with the least possible danger of disturbing the vital currents of the indigenous ways of life. This interesting (and indeed flattering) answer satisfied the whole council, though Chartier, who stormed out at one point, was heard to murmur something about "a monstrous illogicality."

Rumours continued to circulate, of course, about the exact nature and condition of the unseen guests, and many kinds of speculation occurred over the years. It was suggested that they might be black tourists from the new Africa, hidden so as not to shock the local sensibilities. Or that they were mentally challenged adults from the States, who were being flown in at the expense of some generous company charity. Or even that they were highly placed executives of various powerful companies who had come up to this isolated spot with their girlfriends to enjoy their private orgies in an atmosphere free of pollution or of the elaborate climate-controlled environments Americans were by now used to. There were even weirder rumours, fed mostly by the unauthenticated story of some Boy Scouts who had been canoeing in the vicinity of the tourist park, and who had accidentally trespassed into one of the private channels of the river normally hidden from sight by the pyramidal enclosures. These boys, returning home in a rather hysterical state after abandoning their canoe and camping equipment, kept insisting that they had seen giant lizards laughing and chattering and hugging each other in one of the brightly lit recesses under the central pyramid by the river. This was generally scoffed at and was put down to their watching too many science fiction movies. It wasn't the first time this kind of rumour had circulated, but then it was mainly among the younger folks, most of whom had seen such movies as *Star Wars*, *Alien*, and their myriad successors as many as twenty or thirty times.

What became known only to the very few, on the other hand, was that one night someone showed up, at an exceedingly late hour, at the farm now occupied by the Chartier family. Chartier, who had grown very nervous, greeted the visitor with a shotgun and refused to let him in until he had emptied his pockets and agreed to sit across the table and not make any sudden movement in the teacher's direction. The visitor, however, claimed to be talking to Chartier at the risk of his life. He sat there, speaking both English and French fluently, but with a strong Spanish accent, a sallow little man with a dark drooping moustache. He was, he claimed, the contact man of a resistance movement in a well-known Central American country, which he named. While Chartier listened, the man outlined the manner in which his country had been colonized by outside forces, including the notorious Algol Corporation, which he claimed was a completely alien operation, out for maximum profit at any cost. He pointed out how in his country the local economy had seemed to prosper under the influx of foreign money, and how people had bent over backwards to accommodate the activities of the newcomers, including their tourism. Nonetheless, little by little, freedom had been lost, and the promised prosperity had never really come. It turned out that those who played the company game got rich while others lost ground, or failed to rise out of their misery. When protests occurred, the company turned to violence, with the full approval of the government in power. The only solution seemed to be to undertake full resistance, including sabotage and guerrilla actions against the intruders. It was important that the various resistance movements around the world establish contact, since the enemy operated on a global scale. He was proposing that Chartier agree to become leader of the local group.

Chartier was naturally astounded, and had many questions after the first few moments of shocked silence with which he greeted this speech. Like most North Americans, he had never thought of politics in these terms at all, and the idea of resorting to violence to achieve social change had been frowned upon throughout his upbringing and education. All he could say to his visitor was that he would consider his words very seriously, but that he must have some time to think things over. The man disappeared, but as he stood at Chartier's door just before his departure, he made one final dramatic little speech. It was obviously quite sincere but did sound a little exaggerated, perhaps due to the Spanish flavour of the man's delivery.

"There are those who will argue that even to question the right of the tourists to come is a politically subversive act," he declared. *"Yet I predict that partisans living in the woods and subsisting on venison, rabbit, and scraps of garden produce stolen from the visitors will oppose such violations of their environment and native culture, and will gladly pay for their opinions with their lives. They will take for granted that their deaths may even sanctify the evergreen forests, the lake-strewn lands of the north. Perhaps, however, this is only another form of self-deceit; perhaps death sanctifies nothing. Even so, the battle must be considered a righteous one. If you agree, join us."*

Sometime after this incident, which his wife recounted only to their closest friends, Chartier disappeared. There was speculation that he had left out of fear. Some said he was going underground to lead the resistance. His wife protested bitterly that since she had had no word from him, he might have been abducted or even murdered by the company, and she tried to start an investigation. But after some debate, the council decided to shelve the whole business for lack of concrete evidence.

In Easton's Corners, meanwhile, life went on as usual, though day by day the traditional ways were left further behind and new problems arose to bedevil the little community. If the situation didn't exactly add up to complete prosperity, it couldn't be said either that there was a lack of progress in certain areas. As for the visitors, no one ever really caught a glimpse of them, not for certain, and interest was only aroused again when it was rumoured that the Algol Corporation was pulling out its whole operation to relocate in a more unspoiled area of the north. There was quite an outcry then, and many representations from groups of every kind, but still, very few local folks had a bad word to say about the tourists themselves. The feeling was probably best summed up by old Bob McClaren, who had lived through the whole business, had evaluated all the rumours for what they were worth, and had decided that though the tourists might be a little shy, and the company a little greedy, taken all in all they were regular folks who deserved the same fair shake as everyone else.

Arion and the Dolphins

They relate that Arion of Methymna, who as a lyre-player was second to no man living at that time and who, as far as we know, was the first to invent the dithyrambic measure...was carried to Taenarum on the back of a dolphin.

Herodotus, *Histories* I, 23

A few years ago I retired to the country east of Corinth. As you know, the isthmus that bears the same name as that great city touches the sea at Kenchreai on one side and at Lechaion at the other, so we residents are never deprived of the sound of waves, the crying of gulls. Our land belongs to the god Poseidon, they say, but in my time it was Periander the Tyrant, a mere mortal, who ruled us—and with an iron fist for the most part.

I was one of his lackeys, a fortunate one who kept the wheat records and doled out appropriate supplies in time of famine. Luckily for me, the goddess brought us fair harvests for so many consecutive years that my job was easy. I took the usual percentage, but no more, and Periander, appreciative of my restraint, gave me a small farmhouse near the coast to retire to.

Even as I dictate this, I sit on my fine paved terrace, in the shade of a few straight-growing pines, and look down on my olive trees, my kitchen garden, and the rocky path that leads down to the seashore. It was up that path, two years ago, that the man came whom I mean to speak of: Arion, the famous singer and poet, whom I entertained on this very terrace—if you can call it entertainment to have a man blithering and gibbering a mad story at you while you try to calm him down with cup after cup of your best unmixed wine.

"I can't believe it!" he wailed at me. "I can't believe it of my own compatriots. They tried to kill me! They were going to kill me for my money! The swine! I escaped them by a stroke of luck and through my own courage. But it was a close call!"

My wife, Peirene, hearing the racket, had sent the servants out to find out what was the matter. When she learned that a half-mad stranger had dropped in—a poet everyone knew from years past—she came herself and calmly pointed him to the bath, giving orders that he should be cleaned up and restored before the wine I had been dispensing so liberally made him even crazier.

For a few moments he merely stared at us, a round little man, middle-aged and nearly bald, his dark eyes full of terror, his fat lips trembling with the urgency of his story.

But then, coming to his senses, suddenly aware that his fine clothes were horribly torn and filthy, he allowed himself to be led away.

"What is it? Has he been robbed?" asked my wife. She was too young to have known him before he left Corinth, or to appreciate how the poor fellow had declined. The good looks that used to attract both men and women had been undermined by drinking and debauchery, and the fear that lurked in his eyes and distorted his manner would have been unbecoming in a slave of even the most churlish disposition.

"I have no idea what happened to him," I told her. "Perhaps he fell off a pleasure boat, or was waylaid by pirates. I thought he was still off in Sicily, entertaining the court with those dithyrambic songs for which he's so famous. Oh, well! I never cared much for poets, but we'll hear a good story and maybe get a dedication from the famous man himself for helping him!"

My wife smiled and squeezed my arm affectionately in a manner that always delighted me. How charming and sensitive she looked, standing there in the sunlight, such a contrast to the bedraggled poet. It occurred to me that I had been on my way to lie down with her for our customary afternoon pleasure when Arion had come struggling up the path and fallen at my feet.

"It's too hot here," Peirene said, running her delicate fingers along the wooden bench and shaking her pretty locks in a gently admonishing manner. "It'll only make the poor fellow more feverish. Why don't you wait for your guest down near the spring? I'll have the wine and cheese carried over there and send him along when he's respectable."

I kissed her and did exactly as she suggested. I walked down the path to the spring, dipped my fingers in, then splashed my forehead with cool water, after which I snuggled down on the rustic bench we had recently set there—and promptly fell asleep.

Only minutes later, it seemed, one of my servants, Kran, was shaking me, and I was groping my way back to consciousness, inwardly cursing the duties of hospitality and the unexpected arrival of this tiresome poet. Nowhere, I thought to myself, no farm or villa, however remote, is far enough off the beaten track to spare its owners the importunities of the world at large. Oh well....

Arion had been scrubbed and restored and lent one of my fresh gowns—not one of my best ones, thank the gods—and as soon as he had stuffed himself with some fruit and bread and swallowed a few glasses of red wine he started to babble out his story.

"You see, friend Ladas, all this craziness, this mad dream, started to take shape as soon as I embarked from Tarentum, on my way back here to Corinth. Just think of it! I had purposely chosen a Corinthian vessel so as to avoid such a mess, and the captain looked so trustworthy. Why he even recited a few of my verses.... Of course, living here in the middle of nowhere you wouldn't have heard of my success over in Sicily. King Admestus was a great admirer of mine; he absolutely begged me to stay. And if I do say so myself he had a good bargain. My experiments with the dithyrambic measure were almost an apprentice work compared to the things I was composing in Sicily! My God! They positively showered me with presents. I had a gold ring from the king that had been in the family almost from the days of the Cyclopes, and the court ladies—well, I must say, they conferred on me even more valuable presents than their precious white bodies. Oh, I can tell you, it was a great experience. But then, if I recall, you're just a bean-and-grain counter—you wouldn't know anything about the rewards of the divine afflatus."

I thought of Peirene, dressed in one of her simple white gowns, sitting with me at sunset and singing one of the folk melodies of her native town, and I wasn't envious of this pompous braggart, not at all.

"I'd gone west," he continued in the same self-preening manner, "to do some experimenting at a court that would appreciate some new stuff. Periander was getting complacent, so I thought I'd show him what I could do for a real patron. Ah, there were wonderful times at the court of Admestus! I could do nothing wrong in their eyes. They couldn't have been more enraptured if I had been Orpheus himself!

And those women—how they threw themselves at me! I gave a few lessons; I had flunkies and disciples to run my errands for me. I speculated a little in land. As I put it once myself, 'A golden tongue is the prosperity of the poet.'"

I shifted on the bench and helped myself liberally to the wine. The man was really insufferable; if I had to listen to much more I ought to get properly liquored—otherwise I might say something I'd regret. This lout would inform Periander, and who knows what might happen to the peace and quiet of my retirement?

I decided to be as civil as I could, and inquired, "But Arion, what on earth happened to you? Were you kidnapped by pirates, or what? What on earth brought you to our little hideaway, looking like a drowned rat, and with nothing to show for all your success?"

"I'm coming to that. I'm a storyteller, Ladas, remember that. We poets don't just blurt things out like common soldiers or day labourers. By the way, what's the name of your housemistress? She's inordinately charming. I don't suppose you'd fancy appearing in front of Periander with nothing to show for all my time in the west."

I was really angry now. "Peirene is my wife. She's

not a slave but the daughter of a fisherman and though it's true she grew up in a fishing village on the coast of Argolis, as you can see for yourself she has the manner and the intelligence of an exceptionally well-bred court lady. Besides—"

But here I cut myself off, not wanting to discourse on Peirene's sexual charms in front of such a smug and supercilious outsider.

Arion smiled at my heat, and with his fat fingers brushed some thinning hair across his bald spot. "No matter! I'll soon be well enough provided for.... At any rate, as I was about to say, despite my success I decided to return to Corinth. Why? Because I was determined to show Periander what I was really worth. But not only that. You see, I was at the peak of my success out there; things could only have gone downhill. At the same time, Ladas, you must understand that we poets are sometimes gifted with prophetic dreams. In this case I had a recurring dream of falling into some great abyss—a black hole deeper than Tartarus. *Brrrr*...it makes me shiver when I think of it!

"At any rate, the trip started out auspiciously enough. Having sailed away from Tarentum, I was actually getting chummy with the captain and crew—we drank together and I suppose I let slip a few hints about what I had in those fifteen or sixteen heavy coffers the dock rats had lugged aboard for me. But the weather was good, and I kept thinking of how I would set myself up at Periander's court. Days passed, and before I knew it we had sighted Point Taenarus—as you may know, the coast is wonderful in those parts. Yet it was that very morning those scoundrels approached me. Everything had changed all of a sudden, I could see it in their eyes. I'd overheard a few of them making fun of me, I'd caught sight of the captain and the first mate parleying together a little too intensely—but I'd paid very little attention. Now it dawned on me suddenly what they were up to.

"They came at me with knives and clubs and told me to jump overboard or they would kill me. I was frightened—who wouldn't be?—but also outraged. To be betrayed by my own countrymen! At the same time—I want to give myself credit—I was thinking how I could outwit them. I told them, as calmly as I could, to take the treasure, only please to put me ashore at Point Taenarus. (Unfortunately, they talked among themselves and soon realized what I had in mind—that I intended to report them to Periander, to have them hanged.) They insisted that I jump. I knew it was all up with me.

"I made one last request, and they granted it to me. From one of my trunks I fetched the finest of the gowns that Admestus had given me—a gown of Tyrian purple, priceless—and then I took up my best lyre. I prepared myself as if for a concert. Perhaps I had a gleam of hope; perhaps I fancied myself an Orpheus. After all, weren't they wild beasts? I could charm them with the music and make them let me off close to shore.

"It was a beautiful day, calm and sultry. The sea gleamed like a polished metal shield, reflecting only a few faint wisps of cloud. From where I sat, on the highest part of the deck, I could see the magnificent craggy headland of Taenarus. I chose the Orthian measure, the liveliest one—I thought it might appeal to them. They watched me; they listened—open-mouthed and ignorant buffoons, to whom I was condemned to sing my swan-song!

"It was one of my greatest performances, and that's saying a good deal. Women have torn off their clothes and crawled to me for less; handsome boys have prostrated themselves before me for a tenth of what I gave that day. But it wasn't enough for those scoundrels. They looked embarrassed—as the mob always does in the face of great art. They scratched themselves, they milled about, those shifty-eyed wretches, rubbing their bellies and complaining about their dinner. I couldn't help shedding a few tears at their ignorance.

"As I wiped away those tears, I happened to look out at the sea. Then I caught my breath and laid my lyre aside, for something incredible had happened.

"All around the ship a white storm of foam disturbed the water. Great tapered bodies leapt and dived, crisscrossing the ship's path, plummeting down into their waterworld and then erupting in such an energy of quicksilver light and joy that it made me gasp. For a few seconds I forgot my plight, and the sailors forgot their malice. We simply watched the dolphins plunge and leap past us in the sunlight. I gaped and I listened—and I could have sworn, not only that their tiny eyes and odd lips expressed a kind of delight, but that the low whistling sounds I heard then were signals—signals of joy—the mouth of the god opening in nature to thank me for my gift of song.

"Without a moment's hesitation I climbed up on the ship's low railing and leapt into the sea."

Arion paused. I looked at him. A spoiled man, fat and balding, a pompous and self-important celebrity, who cared very little for me and my hospitality, and who had just offered to buy the thing I valued most in the world, my wife Peirene. Yet for a moment this dreadful man had made me forget all that, and I didn't dare to speak right away for fear of holding up his story.

"I fell into a kind of blackness," he continued, "blasted and shocked by the uprushing water. For a moment I hung in the vast sea, my legs spread a little awkwardly, my robes tangling and threatening to drown me. Then something drove with a great force from beneath me; my whole body shook with the shock of this contact on my poor rump. Something lifted me; I was hurled upward toward the light. In a violent shower of water, I was lifted into sunlight, far away from the ship, held aloft and secured by the energy of the intelligent animal that carried me—triumphantly, like a hero of the great games—toward the near shore.

"I remember very little of the details. What I remember is the hiss of water, speed and sound, energy and light—the force of a motion that was irresistible. Not even in my wildest, most abandoned moments as a lover have I ever felt such joy in my legs and my buttocks, such a surge of energy through my whole body. It was like being lifted from death to the highest intensity of life. It was like being reborn.

"When we came near shore, I crawled out of the waves and lay for a long time on a rocky shelf. I slept, and dreamt that I had turned into a powerful horse, Poseidon's beast, that I raced across Greece to Corinth with the speed of the wind. When I awoke, the full moon stared down at me and I thanked the goddess for my deliverance. Toward the morning a fisherman spied me, and, although somewhat awed and frightened—no doubt at my appearance—he picked me up and deposited me a few miles from this very place."

The afternoon had advanced a little as the poet spoke. I sat back, grateful for the breeze that ruffled the edges of the vine leaves, listening to the stream run over the pebbles, hearing the low hum of the cicadas, watching the gulls ride above my little farmstead like white feathers floating high up in the clear air.

I thanked Arion for his story. I might have asked him many questions—I was rather eager to, in fact—but I decided it would not be very polite. We gave him dinner, and the next morning I had Kran drive him to the nearest town, from which, with the gold we had lent him, he could easily get to Corinth.

The gold he never paid back, not in full. I suppose I didn't expect him to. I was rather surprised not to hear from him, though, and was confirmed in my sense that poets were mostly unreliable, while Arion in particular, besides being a self-satisfied poseur, was an ignorant fool who didn't understand the laws of hospitality.

All the same, I couldn't get his story out of my mind. Had he really been saved from death by a dolphin? He'd described it all so vividly that I must confess I almost believed him. The story struck me so much that I couldn't somehow bring myself to tell Peirene any of the details. She asked me, of course, what the poet had to say for himself, but I mumbled something about a tale of shipwreck and left it at that. It's difficult to talk about things that disturb you, and about which you haven't been able to make up your own mind.

Then, a few weeks later, a passing merchant brought us some news. It seems that Periander's court had been set in an uproar by the arrival of Arion, who had boldly recounted his tale about being robbed by treacherous Corinthian sailors. Periander hadn't believed him, but had made him lie low for a few days. When the vagrant ship finally arrived in Corinth, Periander had the captain brought to him and asked him about the whereabouts of Arion. The captain explained he had last seen him, safe and sound, in Tarentum, in Sicily. At which point Arion appeared and made his accusations. Captain and crew were promptly hanged, while some of the treasure, which they had stopped in Epidaurus to hide, was recovered and returned to the poet. He became more famous, and probably richer, than ever.

We never heard a word from him, and yet one day a messenger came with a satchel containing my borrowed gown and a small parcel of coins—the famous coin Periander had ordered struck of a boy riding a dolphin, which has since become so familiar to all of us in these parts.

At that point I sat down with Peirene and told her everything Arion had told me.

When I had finished, she rubbed her hands together, smiled, and looked very pleased with herself.

"I thought that story would go down very well," she said.

"What do you mean, my dear?" I asked her. I was genuinely puzzled; the truth had not yet dawned on me.

"Well, if you remember, while the fat poet was being spruced up so as to look a little less bedraggled, you had a tiny nap, my love."

"Of course I remember. I was very sorry to lose

our afternoon together."

"That's very sweet of you.... But I have a confession to make. I myself am responsible for the dolphin story. The sailors, you see, simply tossed the poor old poet overboard. Luckily for him, he was picked up by a passing fisherman and deposited all in one piece at our doorstep. But I knew that wouldn't impress Periander, so I suggested that Arion embroider it a little. I provided most of the details. I thought in gratitude he might send us a generous gift, so that you could buy that new olive press you've been longing for. No such luck!"

I stared at her, flabbergasted.

"But how—how could you? You mean, the whole thing about the dolphins was just made up? That they perform no such miracles?"

"Oh, not quite! You're forgetting that I'm a fisherman's daughter, and that our village is the centre of the dolphin clan for the whole region. I was initiated into the sacred rites at the appropriate age and I've often gone swimming with the creatures. I can't tell you much more, because it's forbidden, dear. But they do whistle, and even talk—at least after a fashion. What's more, they're extremely intelligent, and full of the most incredible life-energy. Arion is such an idiot—he knows absolutely nothing about what goes on in the true living world. Despite his skill as a singer he could hardly have conveyed half of the real power of those great creatures!"

I laughed then, well and truly. No wonder the fool had wanted to buy her! He knew what a treasure she was; compared with my Peirene, Arion's gold, his fat trunks of loot, amounted to precisely nothing.

And when we were lying in bed that afternoon after our lovemaking, I told her she had made me happy in another respect also: she had confirmed my worst suspicions about the originality of professional storytellers.

Dream Planets

All universes exist without beginning or end in the ultimate arena of time, and each moment we experience exists forever.
Gevin Giorbran

We haven't always lived here. There's another place hidden in the Great Memory, a planet we almost settled on, a place we found by luck or destiny and then lost, or got kicked out of. Once you know that, once you get the vision, you think of nothing else. You remember.

Some say the government wants it that way. They feed this lie to us and make us believe it's true; or permit us to recover real things but only in glimpses, which bedazzle us, and render us still more powerless. They deceive us with our own dreams.

Greg Harris gets angry about it now. "Time's a bastard child and yet everybody has claims on it," he said to me the other day. He works in the next office and designs game sheets for Contel. Once he was a believer, but now he's not so sure. He's turned bitter and thanks me for freeing him from his "illusions." I think it's sad that he takes it that way; yet even he can't shake off the vision. That day in Yankee Stadium is still very real to him....

He and I meet sometimes. We look out through the viewing panels across the city: endless grey towers, murky glass lit only dimly by our nearby sun, the sense we have on this planet that something is about to happen, something about to unfold (although it never does).

No one knows what's going on at the top. There's the government, which occasionally changes faces and the wording of its bulletins and press releases, and which endures the occasional scandal, but is otherwise impotent. There are the Companies, which run things, pushing cars and condos, soap and cereal, and paying for the Enterments, the endless programmed entertainment designed to keep us happy, to stop us from thinking or dreaming too potently in our grim little households.

Most of us live in so-called Solar Cities (where the real sun never shines). The rich—the Govs, Company Heads, Entertainers, and Athletes—live on one or another of the Aspens, full-rigged pleasure satellites that endlessly circle the planet. Most of the population fights it out among the garbage heaps of the Outliers, the polluted deserts that surround us on every side, and that (some say) are growing larger every year. The Aspens dump their garbage down there, and once in a while, for sport, someone drives out from one of the cities to shoot some scavenging dumpies and pick up some of the interesting jetsam.

Now in case you're working up your anger about this, in case I've pricked what's left of your social conscience, let me tell make this clear. From what I hear, life isn't that great on the Aspens either. Sex and drugs, competition and bitching with your peers can only take you so far. The suicide rate has been increasing up there; believers are multiplying day by day.

Yes, it's the Great Memory that keeps us alive, that keeps hope flickering in us. The prophets, who preach about the Expedition, the Finding, assure us that we can be saved from this hellhole, that we can get back in touch with reality. They say that *once upon a time*...and the skeptics laugh.

I was a skeptic once. Have I turned into a fool? You be the judge.

2

It started a few months ago when Harris came over as usual during the lunch break. Rebecca Wells was there, too, and the three of us got into it.

We were a funny trio, I guess, but for some reason we began to talk together, at first all three of us, then Rebecca and I by ourselves. I was a bit reticent, and they were wary of me, afraid I would make fun of them (they were believers then).

They didn't dare tell me the truth from their side of things. But after a while, when they began to trust me—Harris first, and then, in a huge way, Rebecca—they told me their private stories.

We all live and work on the 57th floor of one of Contel's minor buildings—Rebecca and I on one side and Harris on the other—and you might think it was inevitable that we would rap together. But that would be wrong. For years all three of us had been working and relating to other people, and no such confidences had ensued. Is it some kind of fix? One of Contel's neat arrangements? You figure it out.

I should tell you first that all three of us are happily partnered, as they say—and I don't mean that ironically, we really love our mates and value them. They and the kids are about all we've got in this rotten world. All the same, after all these years a certain sense of discovery is lost; inevitably, even love gets routinized. Marriage is the best institution our race has ever discovered, but of course it's flawed as hell because it's located in Time One, though it may have started somewhere else.

Everything in Time One is flawed. That's where the Great Memory comes in.

Greg Harris is a big man, with strong hands and grey eyes that fix on you and make you take notice. He's a few years older than I am and looks much older, his face all mottled and roughened from the solar leakage, of course, but you could imagine he's been warding off blows all his life, facing and taking it and standing up and just surviving despite it all. He's got a fat, lovely woman for a wife, a Ph.D. in industrial psychology, and the full quota of kids—three. And he loves baseball. His Memory is about that.

Rebecca Wells is different. She used to write advertising copy, creating illusions, propping up the system she despises with her talent for seductive words. It gave her an ulcer, that work, but she was good at it, got caught up in the challenge. She told me she felt that out of loyalty to her husband and her little boy she just had to keep at it. Contel pays very well for clever words.

At first, though I liked both Greg and Rebecca, I could barely listen to their nonsense about the Great Memory. I'm an instructor in the Metasystems, working at Contel under the Guild to teach people how to meditate and exercise, how to survive in this world with something like integrity. I teach them how to use my skills and my knowledge without turning me into a guru. I do what the company requires, of course, but I try to add an extra dimension: I work to produce more than well-tuned-up robots. Now if people use what I teach to lift themselves out of Time One, to get in touch with the "other realities," that's their business. My business is to give them hope.

So far so good. I think you understand a little, though I haven't told you what my own contact point with the Great Memory is. Until a few months ago I didn't have one; I wasn't even what they call a

Sympathetic, someone who believes in Time Three without having experienced it.

But neither Greg Harris nor Rebecca needed a prophet to get them there.

Harris is simple: his memory is DiMaggio. He acquired a set of ancient baseball cards and began to study them. Then one day he walked down the ramp and landed on the other world, found himself in the bleachers, at the old Yankee Stadium. (It's a legend, that place, nothing like our new sterilized parks; if it ever existed it was probably more like the old Roman Colosseum.)

And as part of the legend there was Joltin' Joe, a tall, casual figure in pinstripes—Horatius at the bridge. He was patrolling the outfield just twenty-five or thirty yards away from where Greg was sitting. You should have heard my friend tell about it.

"It was wonderful," he almost whispered to us, his eyes going misty as he remembered. "I could smell the popcorn and crackerjack, I could taste the hot dogs. I was riding one of the transitcars, thinking of nothing, then all of a sudden I was in the bleachers at the Stadium with my Dad right there beside me, and some beer-swigging lunatic next to us going crazy every time the scoreboard showed a couple of runs for Boston up in Fenway. 'Teddy's hit one!'

the lunatic would cry, meaning Williams. It was August. The Yanks and Boston were fighting it out for the pennant, and this Chicago game was big, but looking at DiMag you would never know anything special was up. He was cool, as always, with the deep gaze, the lanky ease, the grace of movement when he came back, close, so close to where we sat, to snag one.

"The sun was very hot. Spud Chandler was pitching. He mowed down the Chisox one after another. In the seventh when Joe came up he seemed a million miles away, but we recognized him, we knew the stance, the thin-lipped smile, the glint in the eyes. We knew the swing. Then we saw him hit one, we saw it as few did, from where we sat, that high arching drive that would never appear in any replay, never be seen in living colour, except on that rare planet—my imagination.

"The Chisox left-fielder—who remembers him?—didn't move. He just turned and watched the fans reach for it. The ball landed in the upper deck. The lunatic next to us shut up for once. My Dad just looked at me and smiled. That's what we'd come for.

"I saw that when I walked down the ramp."

Rebecca and I looked at Harris. There were tears in his eyes. He didn't want to leave Time Three, he didn't want to come back to the bleak world we live in.

Then Rebecca began to speak. She has a lovely, high-pitched voice, tuneful and never shrill. There aren't too many women who sound like that. But when they do, you listen.

"I once read about an island called Martha's Vineyard," she told us. "Then, one day, as I was tucking my son into bed, I remembered suddenly how I used to go there all the time. It was—it is—a beautiful island. There's nothing at all like it here. Was that in another life? Was it a dream, a memory of a whole other planet? The name was so special and the landscape so vivid I just couldn't believe it was a fantasy.

"When I walked down the ramp, I was suddenly there, younger and crazy-beautiful (do you believe me?). I'd just been married to this wonderful guy and was ready to settle down after a wild life, a first marriage that didn't work. I'd lost my baby son, my husband, and my job, within a few months. I'd lived too long in a grey northern city (though it was paradise compared to ours) and I'd forgotten what it was like just to walk along a dirt road, to feel the wind in my face, to hear the waves crashing on the bare rocks.

"My new husband took me to the island. We rented a house overlooking a cove (everything was deserted, not like here). One morning while Don was asleep I walked down to the beach. Although it was summer and mid-morning it was chilly. I was wearing a sweater and a pair of slacks, and shivering even so. I wished I'd thrown on a jacket; I wished I'd stayed in bed with Don.

"In a few minutes all that changed. I climbed down some slippery, mist-washed rocks, down to the pebbled beach, where tiny crabs scuttled and the odour of fish and seaweed rose like some intimate ocean smell and made me feel both raunchy and pure.

"I was ready to turn back, to get some coffee brewing, to climb back into bed with Don, when all of a sudden the sun broke through the clouds. I remembered it wasn't early, but mid-morning, and felt the air go suddenly milder, the sand starting to warm up beneath my bare feet.

"I saw a large pool of water left by the retreating tide, a pond in a scoop of black rock, beginning to glint and sparkle with the fire of the sunlight. It was so beautiful, that water, a liquid jewelled light, that I reached down and touched it. It was warm, almost body temperature, so inviting.

"Without hesitation I tore off my sweater and

slacks and tossed them on the sand. I slipped down into the water, letting it wash over my body. I shivered just a little, and then felt the wonderful ease of it, as if my arms or thighs would suddenly melt into the light. I was already getting old, in my thirties. I'd been worried about everything, about youth flying away. I'd become aware of Time. But as that water washed over me, as I felt the delicate tingling across my chest and my belly, I knew I'd never been so at ease, never so happy.

"A few gulls circled in a sky, which was turning rapidly to blue. Not far away the waves crashed, but in my tiny pool everything was still, except the light. My body tingled. I thought of the little boy I'd lost, and I cried. My tears fell down on my skin and into the water, like raindrops from the clear sky. I felt pity then for everything, for all the suffering beings of the world, and despite that, I was happy, for them and for myself.

"Much later I climbed back up the cliffs. It was a beautiful day. Don and I made love. I know my second son was conceived then.

"Did any of this really happen? Well, I do have a husband and a son, and they're wonderful, but I met Don at a vidshop, and there isn't any such island as Martha's Vineyard. Or is there? They must have blotted out the island...."

3

We sat silent for a while, then the two of them looked at me expectantly, waiting to see if anything stirred in me.

Now comes the hard part. When I heard these stories I wasn't in touch with the Great Memory. I had no recollection of a journey to a great good place, of a stopover in wonderland before being dropped into hell. All I remembered was growing up on this rotten planet, trying to make a living, trying to find the truth among the illusions, the programming, the con games.

I looked at Harris and I liked the old bugger. With his gnarled hands, his toughness, and his tender spirit, he made me think of some wonderful uncle that I never had. But it was Rebecca who did it for me. I have to tell the truth about Rebecca.

We'd begun to talk even before she found out I was an instructor in the Metasystems. She even claimed to know that she would meet me.

"I've been meditating," she said. "I asked for someone to come and help me change my life, and I know you're the one."

One day we were sitting in an empty lounge in the Contel Building, when all of a sudden I saw her. Up to then, though I had spoken to her quite a few times, she was just someone pleasant in the foreground. What happened then? I don't know, but I want to be specific about the details, even though they don't seem to add up to much.

I'd forgotten my lunch that day, and she gave me a piece of shortcake she'd made and shared some exotic tea with me. I thanked her, started eating the cake, and then, without warning, everything was suddenly different between us. I looked into her eyes and knew her.

It was as if she'd been revealed to me in an instant. I knew everything about her. I accepted her without question. I realized that it would take time, years, or a lifetime, to get acquainted with her, to become familiar with the endless details of her past, with her history, but I didn't give a damn about that. It didn't matter; all that was unimportant. Unlike others who might meet her, I'd never mistake those details for Rebecca herself.

And it was exactly the same for her, as she told me later.

Is that what you call love? I don't know. Maybe it's something else, something much better.

At any rate we were both suddenly very excited. Words tumbled out; we found we had endless things to say to each other.

We sat in that public place, but in a kind of transparent shell, in a bubble all by ourselves. Outside, things passed by meaninglessly, absurdly: Harris wandered in and began to eat his lunch; a cleaning lady emptied the trashcan; a couple of mid-management types were huddling together.

Rebecca sat and talked, her eyes alight with something. She's dark-haired, tall and slender, with a narrow face, high cheekbones, and strong shapely hands, creative hands. She has a bright laugh and when she's amused by something she has a way of turning her head to one side, half-closing her eyes and smiling inwardly, like a happy female Buddha. She's forty-three now, with a few lines on her face, which has the beauty of a worn, perfect seashell.

She told me about her resolution to quit her job and become a real writer. Later, she showed me some pieces that proved she had some talent. But I didn't even need that evidence; I knew she had talent from the first story she told me. I knew she was a natural.

Of course I wanted to help her. That's my job: to help people do what their talents command. It's a small sop our society allows, to keep the lid on things, I guess. I suppose they figure a few novels or poems more or less, a few paintings or symphonies, will never upset the system. They could be right. On the other hand....

That first time, she didn't tell me about Martha's Vineyard, although I knew she was a believer, I knew she lived a lot in Time Two (dreamtime, the wish-fulfillment place). I also knew that she had more capacity than almost anybody I knew to leap into Time Three, that mysterious planet I didn't quite believe in, the place where the real visions are.

After that revelation I began to see her more and more often. We both wanted it; we even craved it. We talked on the vidphone for hours, or walked around one of the city's labyrinthine shopping malls; we had lunch together. We talked about her work, about art and music, about our memories, about the misery of everyday life on this planet, about the possibility of getting away from it, about the wonderful things we might do together, if only.... Remember, we were both happily married; we decided an affair was out of the question. And we didn't have a lot of spare time. Even so, the only moments that counted were the moments we could sit together and talk, and when it didn't work out we felt deprived.

We realized it was an addiction. She talked it over with her therapist, who cautioned her. I was supposed to know about this pitfall already, seeing that I was a kind of therapist myself. Sure, we were strong, we got it under control; but it wasn't easy. The excitement always came up when we met. And it made everything worthwhile. And a funny thing happened. The more we talked, the more we met and inhabited that magic space together, the easier it was for me to believe in the old fairy tale, the easier it was for me to accept that we—all of us humans—were meant for that other planet, that mysterious other time the believers talked about. In those moments we spent together I felt as if I'd been lifted free from this rotten gravity-bound earth; I almost caught a glimpse of that other place. I almost remembered walking down the ramp and seeing…something wonderful.

It went on that way until the end. Does that surprise you? That there was an end, I mean? You thought we were going to have some transcendent experience together, that we were going to ride away together into the sunset? That we would find some way to be friends forever? Well, remember, this is Time One. In Time One everything comes to an end.

4

One day she didn't appear at work. I was disappointed, but not alarmed; this had happened a few times. When she didn't appear the next day, I began to miss her badly, but still, what could I do? I didn't want to call her flat; I didn't want to hang around there. Even residents are discouraged from standing in our streamlined, camera-watched corridors. Still, I asked Greg Harris if he knew anything. He looked at me strangely and said, "I've been thinking. I've been observing you. We've got to talk."

"Later," I said. If it wasn't about her I didn't want to hear it.

When she didn't show up on the third day, I decided to call her office. I had to register the reason for the call, which I was tempted to record as "loneliness"; instead I wrote "collegial concern," using the vidscripter. There were some flashes as the machines checked on my legitimacy, but finally a clerk-similitude came on and announced that Rebecca had been transferred, that she'd moved to another Contel base, the one in Antarctica.

Antarctica! They had to repeat that one for me. No one moves such a distance any more; they just don't issue the permits. And why had she gone without seeing me? Had she abandoned me for her old dreams, for some new world? But she was my world now.

It was crazy; I couldn't understand it...unless.... I had a lot of questions, but similitudes don't answer real questions. And there was no one else to ask.

I was stunned, and feeling very sorry for myself. I got the number and called all the way down there, not giving a damn about her husband now.

I had some trouble getting through—it always happens when you're feeling desperate—and then a maid-similitude came on and told me that Mrs. Wells wasn't available. I asked when I could call back and the damned maid-similitude told me that my calls could not be accepted, nor would they be returned.

I could have smashed the screen, kicked the bloody monitor to pieces, thrown it through the damned walls at the foul world out there, the world I felt more than ever tainted by.

I couldn't believe that she'd done this to me, cut me off like that without any warning. I went over to our flat, told Jane I was sick, took more heavy pills than anyone should, and was out for the whole night.

The next day I made a token appearance at my

consulting booth. I was determined to find out about the possibility of a transfer; I was crazy with missing her.

At the booth there was a message for me. It had come through the machinery, as even the most private messages did. The text was concise: "*We'll meet again,*" it said. *"Search your memory."* Her name followed, without an address.

I held the paper in my hands and stared at it. As a message from her it was so precious to me, it was a life-line. I was shaken with emotion, almost in tears. I could see her face so clearly, hear her voice, yet she was gone, perhaps forever.

I stared at the meaningless text: impersonal, even arcane words. How did the past, my memory, hold the key to the future? I wanted to hear of her love, of her passion, of her joy in what we had experienced together. What I got was the message of an oracle, the words of an enigma.

I started to crumple the paper, then stopped. I couldn't. I smoothed it out and folded it over. I thrust it into my pocket. I had to keep it; perhaps I had some crazy notion that if I reread it enough times it would reveal some secret meaning, offer me some clue to what had happened to us, put me in touch with her again.

Greg had come looking for me. He led me away into a corner of the big lounge and brought me a coffee. For a while he just sat there, watching me and not saying anything. When I couldn't stand it any longer I turned on him.

"Don't look at me like that!" I told him. I thrust the crumpled paper at him. "She's gone, and this is all I've got from her."

Greg took the paper, read it, and handed it back to me.

"It's hard," he said. "I've been watching you guys. I could see what was happening. I feel responsible too...."

He looked around that bleak lounge as if someone might be lurking somewhere, spying on us. But there was no one.

"It's them, the authorities. The government and the Companies. They've planted everything. There isn't anywhere else. Only Time One, the relentless. They've programmed us with bits of some lost past, with what used to be, before they got control. I never did see DiMaggio, though he must have existed once. They've made him more real to me than my own life. By God, I half believe it yet! You have to give them credit. They're artists all right, artists of the big lie."

He waved at the smog-shrouded buildings, at the murky city. "But this is where we live. This is the reality," he said.

"I don't care!" I shouted at him. I leapt to my feet; I couldn't bear to hear what he was saying. "Anyway, I'm not part of that. I'm not talking about the past! Everything I experienced with her is real!"

He just shook his head, and looked up at me sadly. "Thanks to you I've been able to figure it out. I watched as she conned you. She never stopped selling—and maybe they sold her to you. You didn't notice, but I watched you two fall into it. It was eerie. You needed each other so much. They feed our longings, stir up our desires, that's all the control they require. It's better than any drug, much cheaper and more effective. We do it to ourselves in the end."

I had nothing to say to him. How could he understand what had happened? She had gone away without a word because what was between us had become too powerful: it had threatened to smash our marriages, to hurt those we loved. Saying goodbye would have been too painful. And I knew I would see her again....

5

That night the dreams began. In most of them Rebecca and I clung together, only to be hurled apart by some accident, by some hostile presence. In a few she had harsh words to speak to me. In one she appeared naked, but her stomach was covered with scar tissue, and when I tried to embrace her she whispered, "Don't you understand? Love and death are too close together!"

I had no more dreams after that, but I became so depressed that I was deprived of my licence. The guild ordered me to go to a therapist. The only one I could book was a strange little man, a mutant, who wore large boots to hide what must have been deformed feet. He said nothing, but listened as I told him how I was cracking up, how my wife and child couldn't help me, how the image of this woman haunted me.

I poured out my soul to him, and after the maximum week's consultation, he offered me his analysis: "This is a clear case of trauma, of extreme transference, induced by hyper-suggestion. You have associated too much with the believers, and you are nurturing the fantasy that you have known this woman forever, perhaps that you discovered her on some imaginary voyage to the Other Earth. I've written out a prescription. Rest and the drugs I've prescribed should do the trick. Believe me, dear colleague, it's very foolish to think that marriages, even marriages of true mind or spirit, are made in heaven."

I bought the pills, then threw them away. I convinced the authorities that I was cured, and eventually regained my licence. I thought of her all the time, but in a new way: the pain was milder. I had written down almost ever-thing that she said, and I started to read it over and over in private. Sometimes I would light a candle, close my eyes, and re-imagine the scenes between us, using the dialogue I now knew by heart.

One night, while Jane and my son slept, I conjured up Rebecca's story of the Martha's Vineyard baptism. I found myself going through the experience with her, inside her skin, walking with her step by step as she climbed down to the beach from that house on the hill. I lay in the warm pool with her; I felt the sun, the water, on my body; I soothed my tired bones; peace descended. Later, I was part of her as she walked back up to the house. With her I embraced her husband, and even made love to him. Much later, I felt her baby leap inside me....

The candle burned down. I opened my eyes. I remembered. The experience was so vivid that I nearly cried out. I could see everything: the ship landing, the sliding porthole mechanism, the blinding light and green world of that lovely distant planet. Others walked with me, strangers and pilgrims, fellow human beings who had entered the Great Memory. One by one they strode down the ramp, disappearing into the sunlight with fierce shouts of joy. Yet when it was my turn, I hesitated....

I stood at the top of the ramp and watched her come up toward me, as I knew she would. She had a serious, piercing look in her eyes, but when she came close, almost close enough for me to embrace her, she smiled her quick, sideways smile.

"A Bodhisattva," I thought. "She's come back for me."

I reached out to touch her....

And I have touched her; I will touch her. There's no need to go anywhere. I've rejected everything that Greg Harris tried to feed me. They've conned him, killed him with disillusionment, but I know what I've experienced, what I've dreamed. I've found my perfect moment, not in some fake past but in what must really have happened, or else will some day happen in some other time, or in Eternity. You see, I've been able to enter the Great Memory, where time is cancelled out and where Then and Now are joined together....

Outside, the smog still enshrouds our city; the government and the companies conspire as ever to deceive us. You're thinking how clever they were to entrap me, to reconcile me to this nightmare world of ours by such a trick. Skeptics they want to keep in short supply—so Greg thinks, masking his emotions now with a cynical nod.

I can't prove anything, and I'm aware of the possibility that they've manipulated me with her help. It might be so. It might.

Yes, I'm aware of the possibility, but I deny it.

Nothing as real as our happiness, hers and mine, could be an illusion. Think of your own case, of your own most treasured wish, of that walk you must by now have imagined, despite yourself, down the ramp and into Time Three, where nothing ever changes.

What longing compels you? What figure cries out from your dream planet? *We'll meet again, search your memory.*

Acknowledgements

Several of these stories were published in my first book of fiction, *Tourists from Algol* (Golden Dog Press, 1983), which received excellent reviews in *Canadian Literature, the Toronto Globe and Mail,* the *Toronto Star,* and elsewhere, and was listed in at least one influential survey as a notable book of "metafiction" published during the 1980s in Canada. I would like to thank Michael Gnarowski for publishing the *Algol* volume and for other support over the years, and my former colleague Douglas Campbell for once again applying his superior editing skills to a Ms. of mine.

The subtitle of *Tourists from Algol* was "Stories of the Unexpected" and that theme is continued here. "Encounters in Elsewhen," my present subtitle, seems appropriate for stories that zero in on the life-changing moments of characters mostly estranged from our familiar reality. In common with *Tourists*, *Messages from the Sun* depicts the heroism and comedy in our striving to make sense of an absurd world. I hope that new readers will enjoy the "wide range of form, style and theme" and the "weirdly lit imagination," that some critics noted in the original, and take pleasure in the "lyrically poetic description," and the words "moved around with the abstract precision of chess pieces" also singled out by several of my first readers. My next collection of stories will be very different, but I have had fun playing the game of literature in the story-telling traditions embodied here.

Some of these stories were first published in magazines, including *Anthos, Antigonish Review, The Apalachee Quarterly, Phoebe: The George Mason Review,* and *The Canadian Literary Magazine,* and a couple were broadcast on radio (CHEZ-FM, Ottawa).

Tom Henighan's connection with SF, fantasy and metafiction is an enduring one. His 1976 TV lectures on science fiction were broadcast across Canada. His university course *Brave New Universe* (1981-

83) included 48 television lectures and 600 pages of text, as well as interviews with guest experts on each subject. In shaping his Ottawa-based conferences (1978-83), Tom recruited a wide array of distinctive talents in the arts and sciences, including David Bohm, Gerhard Herzberg, John Chapman, Glenn Gould, Frank Herbert, John Brunner, Edgar Mitchell, Huston Smith, Judith Merril, John Lomberg, Robert Zend, Murray Schafer, and many others, His 1999 book on the writings of Brian Aldiss won the approval of the SF master himself, and has become a basic study on the subject.

Also by Tom Henighan

SELECTED PUBLISHED FICTION
Tourists from Algol ((1983)
The Well of Time (1988)
Strange Attractors (1991)
Viking Quest (2001)
Mercury Man (2004)
Viking Terror (2006)
Demon in My View (2007)
Doom Lake Holiday (2009)
Nightshade (2010)
Storm Warnings (2017)

SELECTED PUBLISHED NON-FICTION
The Presumption of Culture (1996)
Ideas of North (1997)
The Maclean's Companion to Canadian Arts and Culture (2000)
Coming of Age in Arabia (2005)
Vilhjalmur Stefansson, Arctic Adventurer (2009)

POETRY
Home Planet (1994)
Time's Fools (2010)
The Fire Lessons (2016)

Made in the USA
Columbia, SC
17 November 2018